WORTH OF SOULS

Book #3
Worth of Souls series

By
Bonnie R. Paulson

BONNIE R. PAULSON

Captiva Publishing

www.bonnierpaulson.net

Copyright © 2015 Bonnie R. Paulson

Cover design – Ashley Byland from Redbird Designs.

ISBN-10:1-943377-03-0ISBN-13:978-1-943377-03-9

Editing by Grammar Smith Editing

BONNIE R. PAULSON

ACKNOWLEDGEMENTS

Brian – Nothing more to say… but I love you.
Jill, Shelley, and Brooklyn – Thanks for your support. This book grew because of you.
Kammie – Thanks for catching the important stuff.
Mandie – Thank you… I can't even list everything you do.
Survivors – Thank you for requesting another apocalypse-style story from me. I hope you love it as much as I do!

BONNIE R. PAULSON

CHAPTER 1

How could I be sure Rowan wouldn't kill my husband? Or my father-in-law?

I couldn't and that simple fact scared the crap out of me. The main reason I'd run far and fast from the gates of the compound was to seek out Simon Phahn... but the further I got from the fence, the more scared I became that I wouldn't make the distance or I wouldn't be around in case John and Bodey tried to get out and find me.

Leaning forward on a peeling white-ish wicker chair standing guard on an old wraparound porch, I folded my hands. With my head down, I stared at the worn and faded deck. The peeling paint reminded me of simpler times when Dad would notice the disrepair and run to the store to get items to fix the chipping exterior.

The house wasn't mine, but I could pretend. I hadn't had my own home since the one I'd shared with Mom in Post Falls. Where was I now? Did the small section of homes have a name? Or would the small neighborhood be lumped in with a once-famous resort town?

The baby kicked me in my ribs, forcing me to lean back in the chair. The tight wicker weaving creaked with my movement. My back ached. My legs hurt. My breasts pushed against the bonds of my bra. I had a headache that didn't want to stop – probably from not getting enough water.

A few days ago, I had doubled-backed to the compound. I couldn't go very far. Rowan wouldn't stop hunting me, but as long as I didn't go far, he wouldn't find me. Every other day the Jeep roared off down the road and I watched the towers for Bodey to return to his shifts. But when early evening approached, I would make the hour long hike back to the small community of empty homes I'd found and wait for the next day.

Leaving and then not running for help seemed pointless and every night as I lay down by myself, I considered running into the community, begging to be taken back.

But I would wait. I held my growing stomach tight. I could do it. I'd give it one more day and then I would try to find my way to Bayview. One more day.

But one more day turned into two and I found myself climbing trees around the perimeter of the compound. Climbing Tamarack trees wasn't easy, especially with being six months pregnant, but as the only trees in the forest with easily reachable branches not completely covered in needles yet, they were my only options. The needles were newly coming in with spring in full swing and the woods coming to life around me.

When I returned to the neighborhood where the gardens had been left unattended and the greenhouses grew things year-round, or tried to, despair at my situation consumed me. The only real vegetable or fruit I'd found worth eating was rhubarb, bright red-stalked rhubarb. Tart with minimal sweetness, its only redeeming quality was that it was edible.

If something happened to Bodey or John, I could always use the poisonous leaves to finish the baby and me off. Not that I would. I had an uncanny ability to survive.

I chuckled, the sound disarming in the quiet of the afternoon.

Survival was only an accident. How I hadn't died escaped me.

Between Charlie, Rowan, the re-emergence of Shane at the community, and escaping the confines of Freedom Pass into the wilds by myself – at six months pregnant, I should've died sooner rather than later. As things stood, I still might not survive.

Sleeping inside a home had drawbacks. I couldn't hear anything unless I slept by the window. If I wasn't careful, someone would be on me before I could do anything. I'd reached my third trimester and moving quickly was a dream on the wind and not a possibility, unless I was falling. I did that faster than ever.

An ant crawled along the grains in the faded wood, jerking its body left and right as if searching for a way down. The uncertainty resembled my own path when I'd left the community.

Now that I was out, I had to save Bodey, my husband, and his dad, John. But how far could I go without clear directions? What did I expect from myself exactly? I was pregnant and had no food, no way to stay warm. No real logical sense to be honest.

If I really wanted to get logical, I'd just ran, scared of the trade Rowan had suggested, scared that one of us would die for the baby, for pissing off Rowan, for just... being. Just surviving seemed to be wrong.

The muggy late-spring heat seemed out of season. Where were the fresh rains? The cloud cover? I shifted, uncomfortable in skin I shared with another person. I couldn't wait to meet my baby, but if I was completely honest, I was terrified.

What kind of a world was I bringing him or her into? Was it cruel of me to allow it? Would terminating the pregnancy be in everyone's best interest? Or was thinking like that just being selfish again? I didn't know what to do.

I had no one to ask, no one to check my emotions with.

Not for the first time, I bowed my head and murmured to anyone who would listen. "I need help. I need help. Please." What if someone heard my desperation? I didn't even know who exactly I prayed to, but I had nothing else. All of my options were gone.

I could just run. Just get out of there. I had approximately three months left before I would need to get help delivering the baby. Certainly, I could find someone somewhere and be safe by then.

If I ran, though, I'd be leaving Bodey and John. I couldn't do that. I'd already abandoned them to the repercussions of me leaving the compound. They couldn't have known I was leaving, running away, but Rowan wouldn't care.

He'd make them pay.

And then I would suffer. A shudder set my teeth to chattering.

The house I'd chosen had a manual pump out back, just to the side of the greenhouse. One thing Mom had always reminded her pregnant friends to do was stay hydrated. I'm not sure how to tell how well I was doing, but I tried. Even the headache wasn't a for sure sign I was dehydrated. Pushing myself carefully from the chair, I leaned backwards, stabilizing myself with a hand to the side of the small of my back. I wasn't even as big as I'd once seemed, but the ball under my ribs threw off my balance.

Crickets called to me as I made my way down the stairs. A fresh sweet-scented breeze brought a growl from my stomach.

Once I reached the bottom of the steps, I kicked aside the noxious Canada thistle clutching at my jeans. Everywhere I went something clawed at me, people, plants, everything.

Missing my daily showers I'd gotten in the compound, I brushed past overgrown plants encroaching on the handset stone path. Whoever had lived there had taken pride in their home with carefully matching paint on the greenhouse, main building, and three outbuildings, and sheets on all the furniture inside the house.

The homeowners had left, probably expecting to return but not for a long time. I couldn't tell when they'd gone exactly, but with how rundown things had gotten, it must have been more than a winter season ago.

I snuck my hand under my belly, a habit I'd formed and couldn't seem to stop.

A crackling of branches breaking and needles rustling startled me. Where had the sound of the crickets gone?

Past the greenhouse, just on the edge of the clearing of the property, more noises like large animals broke through the undergrowth at a whirling speed.

I waddled to the side, tucking myself into the dark, spider-web decorated corner between the shop and house. Unruly raspberry branches covered me, waving with my sudden appearance among them. They hadn't bore fruit yet, but the slight blossoms and nubs covered the long bushes and I huddled behind them.

Getting eaten by a bear or a mountain lion wasn't on my survival check list. However, I would prefer death-by-animal to the alternative of being tortured and killed by Rowan and/or Shane.

A man's voice, stern and commanding, cut through the peaceful ambience of the home I'd all but claimed as my own. "Check the house. He's gotta be around here."

Not the house. I hadn't left my mark, but I wanted to stay there until I gathered the courage to search for Captain Phahn. And who was 'he'? I had to watch out for someone they chased as well as them?

I closed my eyes, trying to project the idea that if I couldn't see them, they wouldn't be able to see me – like a small child playing hide-and-seek. Were they from Freedom Pass? The voice was familiar— maybe. Groups of people searching for something or someone weren't common. People weren't common. Not so long after the "end."

Footsteps tromped up and down the wooden porch. I had nothing with me to give away my position or that I'd been inside. Even the leftover leaves from the rhubarb stalks I'd eaten were stashed behind tall grasses in the flower garden.

"Nothing, sir." A man reported.

In seconds they thundered past, crashing like locusts traveling through a field. I didn't open my eyes, even held my breath.

And then they were gone. Silence replaced their noisiness. Another minute or so passed and a cricket called, then another.

I exhaled on a whoosh, clamping my hand to my chest and gasping for air. The rhubarb I'd been eating most recently dangled from my fingers. I clenched my fist around it. I had to get out of there. What if they'd caught me? My nostrils flared in fear. What would they have done?

Slipping out the way they'd entered, through the woods, I followed a newly broken in path. Bent weeds and branches led the way from the men and wherever they were headed. If they continued going east, they'd reach Freedom Pass in less than an hour.

If they reached Freedom Pass, I wouldn't be able to return there today. Maybe that was my cue to head toward Bayview – seek help, like I'd originally planned.

A game trail crossed the men's beaten path and I turned, following the thin route through the trees and over logs and rocks. Game trails always led the way to water at some point. I followed the simple route until a wide, fast-moving creek blocked my way. If I did things smart, I could follow the water north until… oh, who was I kidding. I had no idea where Bayview was, except that it was north.

At least I'd found water.

I couldn't go back to the house or houses. I'd probably be better off avoiding human dwellings, unless I wanted to count on the possibility that the encounter with the men had been a fluke, but as close as I was to the Community, the fluke had a higher chance of being a repeat occurrence. With so few people alive anymore, the only thing which made sense was banding together, gathering in for group living.

There was safety in numbers. Supposedly.

Listening carefully in case I was interrupted, I removed my shoes and socks, and scampered up to the top of a moss-covered boulder jutting out over the small pool. Taking a seat on the edge, I swung my feet back and forth, my toes just barely dipping beneath the water's surface.

The frigid temperature didn't bother me. I ran on high heat with the baby and my nerves always on high alert. Birds chirped and crickets sang. Their songs mingled with the babbling of the water.

I had no one to talk to. Even talking to my baby didn't make sense, since I wasn't even sure I could have the child safely. Most of the time I was convinced he or she was going to die – no matter what I did. Plus, what did I say to my baby? Sorry I have no food for you? Sorry to take you away from a warm bed and solid meals and showers?

Sorry to take you from your dad and grandpa?

If given enough time, my thoughts always redirected toward the Christianson men. What were Bodey and John doing? The sun had started its downward trek through the sky so if things were normal, Bodey would be sleeping and John would be finishing up his shift.

But I was gone. I'd run. And they would be dealing with the aftermath of my actions. Not for the first time, I considered running back and choosing Ethan. Rowan's control came from supply and demand. But Shane's... Shane wanted to hurt me for killing his brother.

Who was I kidding? Shane just wanted to hurt me for fun. He would use his brother's death as an excuse.

How had I gotten in the position to have so many men set on killing me for one reason or another? Or, if not kill me, control me somehow?

Too late I noticed the shift in sounds, the switch to just water gurgling over the rocks.

Pulling my shoes toward me, I unrolled my socks swiftly.

"Kelly?" A man's feet stepped into my line of sight, across the water on the other bank.

They found me. Ethan or Rowan or Shane. They'd found me and now I was going to die right there in the center of a beautiful oasis where I'd been stupid enough to stop for a break.

I lifted my gaze, fear slicing through me. I didn't even have a weapon to use at that distance, unless I threw my shoes.

Captain Simon Phahn watched me, eyebrows furrowed as he continuously glanced up and down the creek and over his shoulder. His clothes were wrinkled and worn, but well-kept with patching. He carried a bulging backpack. Most importantly, his cheeks weren't sunken in from hunger or dehydration.

I rushed to my feet, scrabbling from the rock and claiming my shoes and socks. "Captain Phahn!" I pulled up my pant legs and waded across the shallowest point in the water to reach him. Relieved to have found him – even though I hadn't started looking or wasn't even close to Bayview – I stopped beside him and stared. Could he be a mirage? I'd never heard of rhubarb having hallucinatory powers, but I didn't know as much as I could.

He touched my shoulder and ducked down to put our eyes on an even level. "Are you okay? Where are John and his son?" Captain Phahn glanced around again, concern in his narrowed gaze.

The possibility that he would be just like Rowan or Charlie or Shane occurred to me. But if John trusted him, I had to as well. Why was he so far down south? What if Bayview was no longer safe? Desperation welled inside me at the thought. Was anywhere safe anymore?

I shook my head at his question.

His eyes widened and his fingers dug into the material of my jacket. "How? Did someone kill them?"

Realization ran through me. I rushed to fix my mistake. "No, I mean, they aren't dead. I think. I'm out here and they're inside Freedom Pass. I escaped a week ago." A week. Just one week. The seven days wore on me and I questioned how close I was to losing my sanity.

He caught my arm and directed me toward a downed log. Covered in moss and fallen needles, the log protruded from a shale runoff. Leaves and branches from nearby bushes covered the other end.

Handing me a rag to dry my feet, Captain Phahn inclined his head. "Okay, so John and Bodey are still alive?" A pleasant mint odor drifted from him. I sniffed, maybe my headache would go away.

"Yes." I dried my feet then shook off the cloth and returned it to him. "But I'm not sure for how long." Pulling on my socks, I tried breathing comfortably around the baby in my stomach to speak better. "I got away, but that doesn't happen – it's not supposed to anyway. The head guy, Rowan, interviews people who want in. If he takes you in, someone else dies. And he doesn't allow anyone over fifty inside or younger than fourteen or something like that." I rushed on, allowing the terror to leave me in a virulent mess. "He only allows two hundred people in at once. He killed my friend. And her husband."

I hung my head, shoulders sagging. I'd seen enough death to break people. But I couldn't break. I couldn't give into the hopelessness around death. The entire world had converted to discouragement and failure. And death. Rubbing my eyes, I lifted my gaze. "Have you heard anything? Are the governments coming back?" *Will there be relief from all of this pain?*

Captain Phahn stared at me, his mouth slightly open as he took in what I'd said. He shook his head the smallest amount, snapping himself alert. "There's a lot of chatter on the radios, but it's going to be a long time before countries can clean up this mess."

"Oh." Disappointment didn't surprise me. "Were you kicked out of your community?" Why wouldn't he be? Nothing else was going my way.

"No. I came down this way as an ambassador of goodwill. We have an overabundance of some resources and we're severely lacking in others. The council and I decided it'd be good for us to attempt affiliating ourselves with another large community, create a collective of like-minded people." He dropped his gaze to his lap and then looked over the pool of running water. "But we won't want to be aligned with a group that kills to stick to a population number."

Put so simply, the truth had a startling clarity.

We sat together in silence, the symphonic chords of nature swelling around us.

"Did you leave because of the baby?" He pointed toward my rounded stomach.

I nodded, my throat suddenly tight. "He... um, Rowan, he said I had to choose for one of us to die – Bodey, John, me, or the baby." I lifted my palm and tried shrugging off the choice, like 'no big deal' but the pain in the decision choked me and my words came out clenched and broken.

Captain Phahn's eyes glistened and he nodded shortly. "Yep. That makes sense. This Rowan is the leader of the whole camp? It's just him?"

"Yes. Him *and* his son." His son. Oh, what I wouldn't give to castrate Ethan. If he had kept his lustful wants to himself, I wouldn't have been considered for his wife or property or whatever Rowan saw me as for his son.

Captain Phahn watched me carefully, as if every nuance could give him more clues to go on. "What's with the son? You talk like you have a history with him."

I half-shrugged. "The only reason they let us into the compound was because his son wanted me." Heat flushed my cheeks, but he didn't seem to notice. He nodded for me to continue. I breathed deep and ignored my embarrassment. "Things got so bad, that when Rowan said I had to choose between the baby and someone else, he gave me a different option – to go with his son, Ethan." I shuddered. "They're creepy."

"Yeah, that is creepy." He screwed his lips to the side. "We had problems with a previous group in our camp who wanted to control the residents similar to how you're describing – about the time you guys came through and I couldn't let you in?" He continued after I nodded that I remembered. "They wanted to ration food and only allow specific people in, if any."

Captain Phahn picked a chunk of moss from the creases in the log and tossed it into the stream. "While I understand the idea behind hoarding the resources and keeping to ourselves, I don't condone only allowing a specific number of people in or even a specific kind of people."

I drew my knees to my stomach, no way would they reach my chest with the stomach I'd grown. "What happened?"

"After a division of interests with a third of the people siding with them and the rest with my officers and me, we got them to leave. It wasn't pretty, wasn't even peaceful, but they won't be using up our resources or blocking others from joining us. You guys will be safe up there, if you want to give another place a try." He smiled reassuringly at me. How refreshing to be able to sit with another person and not be catalogued as a resource or for how useful I was. He glanced around us once more.

But his community had abandoned others to the wilderness for the sake of the group. What about the individual? "Why is that okay to do? Choose who stays and who goes?" Rowan had taken liberties from his group, taken survival away from even more. Maybe Captain Phahn would have insight as to why.

"Yeah, I understand your frustration. I didn't let you guys in and I'm sorry. But I've known John a long time and I didn't want to bring him in and have him bear the brunt of revolt simply because he knew me from before." He paused, as if trying to figure out the best way to answer my question. "When it's all about surviving, it's got to be about more than just breathing. It's in the living, right? You can live or die, okay, but is that *it*? Is that what we've become? Animals intent on just reproducing and eating and sleeping?"

He shook his head, staring down the valley created by the water then turning to search my face. "Surviving should be more than just live or die – it should be about living justly, living with ourselves. Because at the end of the day, when we look back at what we did or didn't do – we'll need to answer a question on our humanity." Captain Phahn's passion didn't raise his voice, but it clipped his words and strengthened the heat in my chest. "What's the worth of our souls, right?"

His question, phrased so simply, slammed a memory to the forefront of my mind. Mom had confronted Dad and me about where we'd been all morning a few years back. Dad said it wasn't a big deal. He didn't want her to know we had been out buying a birthday present for her. But I said we'd been at the circus and went into great detail about things we hadn't seen.

Mom had looked at me with tears in her eyes and asked so simply, "Is your soul worth a lie?"

The worth of our souls. I'd only ever considered the value of myself as a person, never as more than what I was on the earth. This was my life, right? I only got *one*. Unless, as Mom had repeatedly claimed, we had so much more going for us than the small amount of time we'd been given on earth.

What was my soul's worth? Did I have value? Who decided? Me? Other people? Who? Rowan? Shane? Bodey? Or even Captain Phahn?

"I'm sorry. I feel very strongly about this topic. I think it's why the council gave me the official title of Bayview Goodwill Coordinator." He scoffed at the loftiness of such a plain position. "It's just something to think about, you know? Even as we camp and live off the land, can we still be considered civilized?"

I chewed on the skin of my inner cheek. "Do you think you can still have value, if you killed or abandoned people?" Nobody deserved my details. But I needed to know if I deserved my shame.

He held up his hands, and then tossed from him a blade of grass clinging to his pants. "Hey, I'm not clergy, by any means. But I do have the right to say every instance has a large grey area surrounding a minute black and white spot. Yes, killing is bad, but was it self-defense? Abandoning people isn't a great action, but what was the intention behind doing so?" He glanced at my stomach and softened his tone. "I would think that to save the life of a little one, your intentions *are* just in abandoning someone capable to defend themselves."

My question had been rhetorical, I don't... another lie. I had to make myself realize I was better than that. *Right?* "What are you going to do?" I wanted to lump myself in with him and say "we," but I didn't know him and I wasn't his problem. My baby wasn't his problem. But I owed it to John and Bodey to ask. "I'd originally planned on finding my way to Bayview to ask for your help. Once I got out though, I got too… scared to go far from the compound." Embarrassment flushed my cheeks. "Why are you here by yourself, if things are good at Bayview?"

"Well, we wanted to partner with another group to barter with like I said, but those men who tried taking over are still out here. They must have caught on that I'd left Bayview because they've been chasing after me ever since I headed this way." He studied the ground at his feet and glanced around again.

"I saw some men that way, in a community of houses. I hid when they trampled through. The lead guy was saying something about finding someone." I pointed back the way I'd come.

Captain Phahn studied the trees the direction I indicated. He slowly nodded. "We need to save John and Bodey. That's obvious, right? And I know I can, if I go back for help, but…" He glanced at me, discomfort in the lines of his face and gaze which he dropped to my abdomen and then back to my face.

"But what?" If he could save them, then what was the problem? Why hadn't he left yet?

"I can't just leave you here by yourself. You're pregnant and defenseless." He crossed his arms and watched me, gauging my reaction.

"I've been on my own for a week and I've made it just fine." I didn't mention that the only food I've had is rhubarb and something which may or may not have been currant berries. *At least I hadn't died, right?* "I could come with you, if that's what's worrying you."

"You're right. You've done well, actually. I'm not suggesting you come with me. Actually, I would prefer you come with me, but in all honesty – " Captain Phahn held up his hands. "I'm not trying to be rude or offend you or anything, but I can go faster without you. I'm sure you're very fast, too, but you're *very* pregnant and it's a long walk going by road. I want to take the back way which is almost half the time but twice as hard."

Half the time? And at least he noticed I was *very* pregnant and not just *kind of* pregnant. "I agree. You would be faster without me. Don't waste any time. Just go. I'll be fine." Even as I declared it, I started planning on where I would go to avoid detection and get something to eat.

"I'm not leaving you unprotected. You aren't even in safe from the environment." The man was good at stating the obvious, but his concern warmed me. My aloneness didn't seem quite as stark with someone else worrying about me.

Gruffly, I said, "You're wasting time." I pulled on my socks and shoes and stood, pushing at the small of my back to relieve the tension building just below the curve. "I can make it another couple days. You'll return soon and then we can go get Bodey and John. I'll be fine once they're free."

Standing with me, Captain Phahn watched where he placed his feet. "Let's find a place for you to stay first." He led the way down the game trail I'd followed earlier, holding back a low-hanging branch for me to pass. "I passed a small collection of caves and outcroppings you could stay in while I'm traveling."

A cave. Great. But just because I was safe, didn't mean I'd survive. I had no water, no food, and no way to stay warm. I didn't voice my concerns, and instead followed as closely as I could with pressure on the front of my hips from the baby.

Going downhill was going to suck.

BONNIE R. PAULSON

CHAPTER 2

Surprisingly, the caves weren't too far away.

Up a slight hill, boulders grouped together in the middle of a copse of trees as if someone had taken "build a solid foundation" seriously. Bushes with dark green and neon green new growth sprouted from beneath the bend in the rocks and covered the openings to the caverns. Cool air whispered around the bushes and the leaves twirled in barely perceptible dances.

In a small hole to the side, just off the game trail, Captain Phahn pulled me to the mouth and pointed back down the path. "I'm going north, following the water. There should be some jerky in my pack and two water bottles. You might also find crackers and an MRE or two."

I glanced behind him. A second smaller backpack stuffed to within an inch of its seams bursting hid in the dark corner. Glints on a two-inch carabiner gave away its position and outline. "I can't take your stuff, Captain Phahn." The thought of jerky after days and days of rhubarb made my mouth water. I wouldn't argue with him much over the offer, but I wouldn't feel right taking his resources to survive. Crossing my fingers, I silently prayed he had more food in the backpack he carried and the second one was extra.

He patted my shoulder, ducking his head to fit under the lip of the opening. "Kelly, you can call me Simon. I'm no longer captain of anything, but thank you." The weight of his hand on my shoulder brought tears to my eyes – not pain-filled, but more like wistful. I hadn't been able to speak to anyone in ages. "You take it. I'll be back at base in no time, less than ten hours. The pack I have has some food and I can load up again in Bayview. If I need more than I have, I can get water from nature and some other things."

Relief he would be there and back in less than forty-eight hours comforted me. While hunger gurgled in my stomach, fatigue had been replaced with the presence of hope. "Thank you. I really appreciate your help."

"Thank me when I return. We haven't gotten those men out of there." He read the sudden worry in my eyes and rushed on. "We will, we just haven't done the job, *yet*. I'll come back here as soon as I can with help and more food." He touched his forehead like tipping a hat and walked down the path.

He disappeared past some long evergreen branches, the feathery tips of newer branches moving as he went. The absence of noise didn't surprise me so far from the water. When the resources got loud, so did the animals.

I ducked further into the slight decline of the rock, the back of my head grazing along the bumpy surface. Crouching beside the bag, my hands shook with anticipation. Food. MREs – the closest thing to a meal I would see for a while. If he had the ones that self-cooked, I would be in heaven. One time, John had found some in an Army Surplus store and mine was lasagna which reminded me so much of the homemade version, I could've cried.

Spaghetti with meat sauce tempted me in the entrée packet. Blueberry cobbler? Skittles? I closed my eyes and crushed the MREs against my chest. "Everything is going to be okay, baby, we're going to eat something. Yes, we are." A notch in the plastic of the MRE was placed to help open easily. I curved my fingers into position.

"NO!" Captain Phahn's voice echoed off the rock around me.

Shoving the bag back into the pack, I tucked myself into the darkest corner of the cave. I searched with wildly roving eyes for the man who had left moments before. Bracing my hands on the gritty wall behind me, I ground my teeth together. *Don't scream out for him. Don't call out.*

But I wanted to. Almost like I needed to. I opened my mouth, scuffing my foot forward as if to step out of my hiding place.

His next yell cut me off. "Kelly, run!"

Run? I tensed. I was stuck like a dang jackrabbit in a trap. There were no other exits except the main one and based on the nearness of his voice, he was right on top of me.

Grunts and thuds filled the air. Material ripped and a muted cry awakened my fears further.

Where could I go? The cave wasn't huge, maybe ten feet deep and seven across. The opening didn't gape or anything, but it was wider than a normal sized door in a house. Because of the leaves from the bushes in the way, I couldn't see anything happening – only green leaves and brown twigs and branches.

"Check for the girl." Ethan's voice carried the distance to me. I had to make a run for it, before whoever he sent caught me.

I zipped the pack and drew on the straps. Ethan's obsession might get me killed.

The bang of a gunshot suffocated me. Startled, I ran like a pheasant from a field. I didn't even look where I was going, just ran headlong out of the cave – right into the guard's arms. His eyes widened when he recognized me. The same guard who had let me out, who had wanted to walk me into the woods the day Shane stopped me. His dark features gave him away with deep brown eyes and close-cut curly hair.

He held me in a bear-hug and cradle-walked me to Ethan and a downed Captain Phahn. I tried jerking from the guard to get to Simon, but his hold was too strong combined with my hunger induced weakness and lack of solid sleep.

Ethan watched us approach. He couldn't hide his glee, as he hopped from one foot to the next, his gun aimed at Simon. A twinkle in his eye sparked concern when he threw his head back and crowed like a rooster. "Take that!" He danced a little jig and sashayed closer to me.

Once the guard had me within reach, Ethan grabbed my bicep and jerked me to him, lowering his gun. His breath hot on my face, he murmured, "So happy to be the one to find you, Kelly. Did you miss me?" He leaned close, inspecting my skin. The next instant, he licked my cheek and I jerked back.

Without looking at the guard, Ethan motioned down the path. "Grab the old man, let's go."

The guard pulled Simon to his feet. A large red spot on his jeans above the hip pocket worried me. The location was too close to the same spot Mom's gunshot wound had been. And she'd died. I searched the captain's face, his features tight and pale. He stared at me, as if trying to telepathically give me a message. But I wasn't good at understanding facial expressions or even lip-reading.

Ethan yanked me around to follow him. His grasp enclosed my wrist, rubbing my skin painfully, I had little room to maneuver for escape. Where before the forest had been so appealing, I found the nuisances as every root jutted from the ground to trip me, every thistle clung to my pant legs, every rock seemed covered in moss for me to slip on, and Ethan pulled ever onward.

I glared in his direction as I straightened myself after another near-complete stumble.

He'd driven the Jeep and hadn't parked far from where we'd hidden by the caves. Pushing me into the front seat, Ethan clipped the seatbelt shut and leaned close. I tried leaning away in case he licked me again. "If you try to escape, I'll shoot you in the stomach." The baby. How dare he threaten my child? I ignored him, staring straight ahead, arms crossed at my waist. The man had better be careful before he calls out mama bear. Idiot boy.

I rolled my eyes. "Then I would die and you couldn't have me."

The four-door Jeep filled up quickly as the guard and Captain Phahn climbed in the back. While Ethan ran around the front of the vehicle, I glanced over my shoulder to my new friend. He met my gaze and nodded his head the smallest amount, flicking his eyes toward the backpack I'd worn.

I couldn't get any of the contents to him at the moment, but maybe he had some kind of weapon inside or something. I didn't remember a gun, but his coat had enough pockets, it wasn't impossible if he carried.

After Ethan climbed in, I couldn't help myself. I had to know, so I asked, "Are we going back to Freedom Pass?" The name brought bile creeping up my throat. Nothing about the place was free and forcing myself to stoop to talk to Ethan made me ill.

"Not yet." He reached over and pinched my leg above my knee, allowing his hand to stay there and rub up and down my thigh. I tried pulling away, but there was only so much room and so far I could move with my stomach and aching back and hips. He clenched his hand down on my leg. I winced. He muttered, "Stop trying to get away from me. We're meant to be together. Just give into it. Things won't hurt as bad." He winked at me and then released my leg.

Off-key, Ethan hummed *My Girl*, a very old song Rowan made us listen to some nights when I stayed in the compound. Like a scene from my mom's favorite old movies. I wanted to scream at Ethan that we weren't on a date and I wasn't his girl and no matter what he wanted, I wasn't going to do it.

Oh, how I missed my husband. I turned and stared out the window. I hadn't been in a moving car in so long. The last time I'd been in a vehicle, I'd cuddled up next to Bodey in a rainstorm, our bodies heating each other while we'd waited for a sign John was safe.

Where was my husband and why hadn't he escaped yet?

Okay, the last part was unfair. There was only so much he could do – anyone could do.

I'd lucked out escaping when and how I did. But enough was enough. I needed him back and safe.

My reflection in the window had a rounder face than I remembered, like I ate better than I did. Beyond my features, trees and rocks whizzed past. We bumped and jostled down a dirt path... I didn't want to call the path a road, because that would suggest it was easily passable. There was nothing "road" about the trail we were on.

The right tires went up three feet on one side as they climbed the varied angles of the path, while the left stayed on the more level ground. I grabbed the overhead handle and closed my eyes, holding my stomach with my free arm. Oh, my word, was that me that stunk? A whiff of body odor hit me when I lifted my arm, begging me to drop my hand out of embarrassment.

Seven days without a shower…

Simon grunted. The bumping couldn't feel good on his wound. I hadn't even had a chance to look, but any body shots weren't classified as desirable for a reason.

We bumped down the trail for eons and years and decades, and oh my word, when was it going to stop?

And just like that, the bumping from hell stopped. I patted my stomach, around the navel and down by the pubic bone. Everything seemed okay. I slowly opened my eyes, watching as Ethan bounded down from the Jeep and rounded to my side.

He opened my door. I shrank from his clutching grasp as he reached for me. His face darkened and he roughly yanked me from the seat. "You'll learn to like me." But something in his tone told me even he didn't believe his words.

I know I didn't.

We reached the door and Ethan stopped, letting the guard push Simon through first. Ethan turned me toward him, his touch suddenly gentle as he grazed my cheek with his thumb. "Just think, Kelly, we could rule our own community. You and me. I've seen how calm you can be. You would be my rock and I would be your hero. Let me. Let me love you." With both hands, he framed my face, the bulk of his palms under my chin. Tilting my face up, he pressed his lips to mine.

I closed my eyes, grinding my lips together as hard as I could against his invading tongue. He dug his thumbs into the soft skin under my chin and I opened my mouth to cry out. Taking advantage of my vulnerability, he shoved his tongue in my mouth. The hot wet invasion gagged me as he tried tasting all of me.

He pulled back, satisfaction glowing in his eyes. "I told you, you'd like it." He dropped his hands and I breathed, wiping at my lips and grimacing.

If anything would bring on morning sickness, it would be another one of those.

"Do you want me to carry you across the threshold?" He reached down and slapped my butt. I hadn't felt so materialized in a long time.

"No, I don't. We're not married, remember?" I grabbed the straps of the backpack to steady myself and hold back the punch I wanted to deliver.

But Ethan was unstable like a weighted ball on a crooked surface. Physical contact of any kind might encourage him. Or, yet again, if he felt threatened or whatever by me, he might take his insecurity out on someone else, or me, or worse, my baby.

He shrugged, his grin like that of a small schoolboy. "It's only a matter of time until you're mine, Kelly. Why fight me so hard? Plus, Bodey isn't much. He has nothing. Is nothing. You could be with somebody important." Ethan opened the door and guided me through with fingers on my elbow. His manic mood swings made me dizzy as he slapped the side of the wall and grabbed the side of his head. "Why won't Dad just kill them already? It's not like we need them." Ethan kicked the side of the cabin, yanking me roughly forward and then coming to a stop.

Wait! Bodey and John were alive? If only for a moment, I would kiss Ethan again to hear more – how were they? Did they miss me? Were they in trouble? So many questions, but he'd only let the information slip. He wouldn't be interested in anything other than him and me. His manic moods dimmed the hope his words gave me.

Sidestepping from Ethan's instantaneous rage, I blinked at the sudden darkness. Small circular holes had been cut out of the walls, large enough for a gun muzzle to get through and see around, but that was about it. The holes didn't lend much light to the small cabin, but enough to see by. My eyes adjusted to the dim interior and the sight of three other people standing against the far wall with their faces pinned to the rounded logs startled me.

At least we wouldn't be alone.

Simon made it as far as the wall beside the door before he collapsed onto the ground, landing on his uninjured hip and side. I rushed to kneel beside him and to escape Ethan's touch.

Ethan glanced around the cabin, his eyes landing on the other occupants. He turned a glare to the guard. "Outside, now."

The guard followed Ethan out the door, both of them coming to stand beside the opening. Neither of them closed the rickety, dark brown panel.

"I told you to get rid of those people." Ethan's angry words shifted the tension and fear in the room to a discomfort unrivaled by anything else. Seriously, how did you sit beside someone whose death was being discussed like a paper that hadn't been turned in on time?

"I haven't had a chance to do anything. I've been looking for *her* with *you*." The guard's bitterness dripped from his tone. "Why aren't you taking her to Rowan like he ordered?"

"Yeah? You're on *Rowan's* side now? Really it's none of your business." Ethan's voice rose to a high pitch which made me squirm. "How about this? You get to stay with them, until they're dead. Once you've completed your job, then you can come out. And I'll do whatever I want with the girl." Ethan drove the man inside, thrusting his finger into the guard's face. "And don't touch her." He slammed the door, a grinding on the other side when he drew the bar across to lock us in.

Don't touch me? Hypocrite couldn't keep his hands off me.

The guard stood at the door, his shoulders heaving. He shook his head, not moving other than that.

Two men and a woman turned from the wall, facing us slowly. The woman watched us, circling around the room as if she'd seen us before, but couldn't approach more directly. The men plopped onto the ground, leaning their backs against the wall and staring into space. All three were older, but not what I would describe as old. I hadn't seen an "old" person in years.

The woman's long silver-streaked brown hair was matted, but pulled back in a braid trailing down her back. Her jeans hung loose on a thin frame. Strong shoulders squared her shape instead of giving into the rounded look so common on women from slouching. Bright blue eyes watched me as she approached, slowly. Her gaze shot to my stomach and then back to my face, questioning.

As interesting as she was, Simon's condition wasn't improving. His ragged breathing scared me. Laying on the ground, he straightened his legs, letting the toes of his boots fall outward into an elongated V. He closed his eyes, ignoring the dirt floor and the straw as it poked him in the neck and head.

Shuffling toward him and kneeling, I bent toward his chest, tucking my arm beneath his shoulders and back. "Come on, let's see if we can get you to sit."

He nodded shortly, the effort obviously energy-sucking. He hissed when he reached half-way up.

The guard spoke, his volume subdued but clear. "Don't bother. None of us will make it out of here alive."

"I didn't ask you." Focusing on Simon, I rolled him to rest on his side, wound side up. "Do you think it'd be okay, if I look at the wound? I did medical at the compound." In our situation, he didn't need my credentials, but I wanted to validate myself, give myself more expertise than I felt like I had at the moment.

Because right then I felt like nothing more than a scared, knocked up nineteen-year-old alone with other prisoners held by a psycho.

Oh, wait. That was actually my reality. Validation wasn't needed.

"Of course," he whispered, his lips tight from the pain. He winced as I pried the shirt from his waistband and tugged his cargo pants down lower on his hip. A nice clean entry point camouflaged the jagged exit wound in the back. Angry flesh bled onto his thick jacket.

Pulling off the backpack, I dug around, searching for extra material. A pair of wadded up socks would do. Shoving the socks against his back,

I tried not to grimace, but hold a calm expression. I'd never been good at hiding my emotions, but maybe the situation would warrant the semi-panic screeching across my features. Either way, what my face showed didn't matter, because he faced away from me and I didn't have good or bad news to give him.

The woman studied my face. "Is everything okay?"

"Sure." I held the socks tight to his wound. "I need to get him a poultice but we need him to stop bleeding first." Cammie had used poultices and compresses on everything. I couldn't remember all the ingredients but she'd urged me to remember some because one or two was better than none.

"We don't have anything in here, except a little rain water to drink." She rubbed her arms as if suddenly chilled.

I glanced around the sparse room. A table lay on its side, legs broken off, one shoved through a hole in the wall. Red-tinged fingernail scratches in the door and around the holes painted a picture I wasn't ready to assimilate. "What about food? Doesn't he feed you?"

The man furthest from me snorted. "Food? Why would he waste food? He wants us to die, he just can't bring himself to pull the trigger." He jerked his thumb toward the guard still standing at the door. "He has to have some poor schmuck do it."

The man raised his voice and glared at the guard. "Right? He has to have you do it and you can't, because you're the one who let us in the stupid camp in the first place." The man huffed, sitting back, adjusting his shoulders. "Talking about some great place with food three times a day and music. Where'd you go when they kicked us out and we had to wait for you for seven hours – locked between the fences?"

Turning around, the guard nodded jerkily. He swallowed, watching us each with wide eyes, the whites clear in dark. "That's my job, to let you in. I didn't know they would kill you if they didn't want you inside." He offered a lame shrug and a half-smile. "Once I let you in, I went back to my own bunker because my shift was over. I didn't even know you were waiting that long."

The guard's smile angered me. I held pressure to the exit wound and pushed with my bare hand to the front. I didn't have enough extra material to bandage the front too. I shook my head, settling onto my rear end while administering to Simon.

When I finally started speaking, it was quiet but I built in volume. "Rowan has been killing for quite some time. People go missing and the residents don't say anything because they like their food and their homes. You have *some* power with your gun and your position. You're no better than him or Ethan when you do *nothing*."

"I have one gun. They have lots. You should see under the warehouse. More guns than I've ever seen!" He shouted. The slight echo of his words bounced back at him and looked down at the floor. "Look, now I'm one of you. I want out, too." Hard to take him seriously when we all knew the only way he was getting out was if three people died.

The silent-to-that-point man leaned forward on the ground, his eyelids droopy. "The only way he's going to let you out is if you kill us." He looked at the rest of us, nodding toward the guard. "I say we kill him and eat him. I haven't eaten in so long and he looks like a good piece of steak."

Before things had turned worse and the bombs had dropped, my mom and I had discussed the possibility of cannibalism. Then, when our fridge had been full of food and we ate three to four times a day, the thought had been repulsive. But as I sat there, having not eaten well in a while, I could see the appeal. My dad had once laughingly claimed people would taste a lot like pork, because the diets were similar.

I hadn't had bacon in a long, long time.

Shaking my head at the turn of my thoughts, I laughed to lighten the mood. "We could, but we don't have a fire and I'm not eating anything – or anyone – raw."

The guard hugged his waist and sank to the ground by the door. He whimpered, closing his eyes and staring hard at the swirls in the dirt.

"Since we won't eat you, you can answer our questions instead." The woman moved toward him, her mouth set in a thin line. "First, what's your name?" A civilized question for a man who might not deserve civility. But I couldn't begrudge her the politeness.

He nodded curtly, leaving his eyes closed until he spoke. "Mike." He pulled his knees toward his chest.

The woman moved closer to me and the downed captain. "Okay, Mike. I'm Dana. The men over there are Lance and Gary." She pointed at me and Captain Phahn. "They're new, so they can introduce themselves." She inclined her head my direction. Something familiar in the way she held her chin and the tilt to her eyes.

To be honest, I didn't want to introduce myself. Dana could be civil. Simon's blood spilled onto my skin because of the actions of Mike. Why did I have to play nice? I took a moment before answering, collecting my anger into little bundles in my head to deal with later. Quietly, I did as Dana suggested. "I'm Kelly and this is Simon." I had so many questions, I wanted to spout at him, but I held my tongue until Dana's directed interview allowed.

"Kelly and Simon, nice to meet you." Dana smiled at us and then turned toward Mike. "Don't you think it's nice to meet us, Mike?"

Had everyone gone loopy? Who cared if it was nice to meet us? But her questions and the mannerisms she'd adopted calmed the room. While everyone was still hungry, no one looked at Mike like a meal – hard to eat your steak with you remembered it as Bessie. My dad had a lot of good one-liners.

Mike nodded jerkily, his eyes darting from side-to-side as he focused on each of us. "Yes, nice to meet you." I bet.

Dana stepped a little closer to Mike as if establishing a private conversation. She spoke slowly. "I'm very hungry, Mike. Did you happen to bring any food with you? Three days is a long time to go with nothing but water." Her tone was even, but her hands shook at her side.

Before Mike could answer, I spoke up, asking the men and Dana, "How long have you been in here?"

The man Dana indicated as Lance raised his hand limply from his knee. "Six days." His wariness made sense. There were no safe places to rest their heads or even to sit properly.

Gary avoided looking directly at me, except to cast skittish glances at my stomach and Simon's wound. "Five."

Dana held up four dirty-smudged fingers and her gaze returned to Mike. "We're hungry."

The guard didn't answer, just stared at the ground. Where had the manners gone?

Sliding the pack off my back, I reached inside and pulled out all the food I could find and spread the contents out beside me, just behind his back. His chest rose and fell. I assumed he slept, which should be a good thing, but I wasn't sure. Mom had fallen in and out of sleep with her injury. She'd bled out and I just couldn't let Simon do the same. Mom hadn't lived long enough for me to worry about infection, but Simon would and I would get to deal with it in all its troublesome glory.

But what could I do? "Here, we have to share and I'm not sure how long the supplies will last, but there's some in here for everyone, if you want it."

Gary and Lance moved slowly toward me on their hands and knees. Their weakness from hunger more apparent as they moved. Could I be happy that they'd had water for the last three days?

Dana walked to me, but lost all grace when she lunged for the floor, grabbing up a bag of jerky and ripping the plastic open. She handed meat to Gary and Lance and then tore into the strips with voracity.

Embarrassed at their base need, but understanding it, I cautiously pulled the peanut butter packet from the abundant pile of food and ripped the packaging open. Eating the peanut butter plain with one hand, I held the makeshift dressings to Simon's wounds with my free hand and my knee. I needed to eat and the prisoners' desperation dragged at me, reminding me how close to the same emotion I was.

"Can I have some?" Mike watched us, his eyes narrowed, as if worried we would eat all the food.

Dana and the two men didn't even acknowledge his request. I figured it would be safest to do the same. What if I offered him something and the other three turned on him and I like a pack of hyenas? Safety-wise, not giving in to his demands would be the best bet.

Since no one else seemed interested in asking him questions, I didn't hold my tongue anymore. My questions pressed at me from my heart.

"How are Bodey and John? What's happening inside?" I glanced at Dana when she stopped chewing and stared at me, then back at Mike's face. "Did Rowan hurt them? Are they…" I couldn't say what I should. Couldn't ask if they'd been killed. As much as I wondered and thought their murders were possible, saying it would thrust the concept out into the universe and might make it happen. So I held my fear close to my body, not wanting to say the words, but having to ask anyway.

"Freedom Pass is falling apart." Mike unfolded his arms and glanced toward the hunting hole-sized windows. By the time we were done in there, Mike's fingernail marks could be on the walls, too.

"What do you mean falling apart?" If he didn't get talking, I would consider feeding him to Gary and Lance.

"What do you think I mean? Your disappearing *stunt* triggered something, like a revolt, but worse. People aren't working because no one is in the clinic to take care of injuries or illnesses. Rowan tried shuffling things around, but no one likes the job in there or even knows what they're doing. The morning you left, John went to his shift at the shop and told the other guys there you were gone and why. They dropped everything, grabbed up tools for weapons and stormed Rowan's place." He shook his head, disbelief slowing his pace. "They destroyed everything they could reach."

I didn't care about all that. His mundane details didn't matter to me. "But what about Bodey and John? Are *they* okay?" Watching him, I ignored everything else around me. I had to know.

Because the only thing holding me upright and hopeful was the fact that Ethan had said they were alive.

But what if that just meant, they hadn't died… Yet?

CHAPTER 3

Mike continued talking like I hadn't interrupted. "When everyone found out you were pregnant – nice job hiding that by the way – and that Rowan had said you had to choose for one of them or yourself to die, I think that broke the complacency for everyone." He shrugged, avoiding eye contact with everyone but me. "Well, most people. Some just ignored it. We've had nothing but problems since that day."

"It's only been a week." I scrunched my forehead, perplexed that my simple absence could cause such turmoil. Nobody even knew me, let alone cared about me enough to begin a revolution in my honor.

Mike lifted his head, his eyes hard as he thrust his chin forward. "A week from hell. Rowan stopped anyone from being brought in and just wants everyone killed until he can get this under control."

He shook his head, his shoulders hunched as he tried to keep himself protected against the door. "If you ask me, there's no controlling this. He wants us all to bring you in so he can show everyone you're alright and not dead like they all think. Then I bet he has you killed. He hasn't killed your men yet because he's worried about furthering the revolt." He shifted his eyebrows and rolled his eyes to the side.

Oh yeah, he would definitely have me killed. I picked at a chunk of jerky, forcing myself to taste the salty end. Until Bodey and John's fates were a certainty, my appetite might not return. "Why do people even care? Nobody knew me." And they all stayed away from me, like a pariah or something. Even Cammie had been slightly reserved at times, as if she expected me to disappear any moment.

Dana listened intently. She answered for Mike. "Because pregnant women are special. There's something about them even infants don't have. There's like a hope or something wrapped up in a woman pregnant with a child." She smiled softly at me, glancing at my growing belly.

"How many guns does he have? You mentioned a warehouse of weapons." Simon's question crept quietly from his spot on the dirt floor. *Thank you, Lord, he's awake and sounds lucid.* I repeated his question for Mike.

Eyes lit up on the topic which wasn't so personal, Mike replied, "He has a whole warehouse full."

"What warehouse? The only one there is the food warehouse." I watched Mike. Maybe Mike lied. He hadn't said anything about Bodey or John.

"The weapons are under the edible inventory. Rowan has so many. Did you know the compound used to be a stopping station for military? They abandoned the concept a few years before the War." Mike knew more than he let on. His knowledge just might save him from being eaten alive – if he provided information about Bodey and John like I needed.

"Answer her question about the men." Dana had been listening. I appreciated her help.

Mike sighed, folding his hands between his knees. "They're in containment. I haven't seen them, so I have no idea what their condition is but I can't imagine it's good. Rowan goes in to see them every day and there's usually some..." He glanced at me, then toward the wall. "There's usually some screaming." He rushed on when I gasped. "But it's never very long and I think he's just trying to get some information."

"Why can't he just let me go?" My hands shook, but I knew why. Charlie had been similar and Shane. The crazy ones would be the ones to survive to make the rest of life hell for those of us just seeking something safe and secure. With so few survivors, they would be able to focus on someone like me, someone who normally wouldn't merit attention but without competition, I stood out like lightning on a dark night.

"Psh. A revolt started because of you. People took notice. I don't think that's coincidence and well, you've seen Ethan. He's like a rabid dog. He won't stop. Something is wrong with his head and Rowan gives him whatever he wants. Too bad for you, and all of us, you're what he wants." Mike glared at me. "Why not just go with Ethan and stop this? Freedom Pass was okay, it was safe, you know? Food and water. You had to go and get greedy."

Fluttering in my stomach along the outer perimeter grew with my anger – the baby sensed I was upset. "Greedy? Wanting safety without fear of death from *anyone* is considered greedy? What is wrong with you? Is Rowan slipping you guys something in your drinks?" I thrust my lower jaw to the side, staring at the man like he'd lost a few marbles. Maybe he had. What type of person put themselves above others, wrong above right?

The classic survivor did. The person who would do anything to stay alive.

Me. I would've done the same thing not too long ago. With my headlong flight from Freedom Pass, I still felt like I had done exactly that – put myself first. But my intention hadn't been to harm others, or make things harder. My intention... had been to save my family, my baby, my husband and his dad. And me. Lastly me.

Was it so wrong to want to stay alive? Did my desire to survive make me the same as Mike? The same as Rowan and Ethan? Or could I say I had some of the captain in me – integrity while not dying? Living with something to be able to look back on without guilt, without shame.

Mike continued speaking, breaking through my musings. "Ethan locked Rowan up on a pretense, like he was taking over. So Ethan does what Rowan wants and the people trying to revolt are somewhat assuaged thinking he has his own agenda. The only ones who know are the guards. We do what we're told." Sadness covered his words and he pushed a rock around on the ground with one finger.

"What are they going to do with everyone? Kill anyone who's against them?" I bit my lip. If that was the case, then John and Bodey didn't stand a chance. In fact, they'd probably be first to go. Unless, Rowan wanted me there to see the mess I'd caused and to see the consequences. The man had lost his mental capacity, so who knew what was going through his head.

Scoffing, Mike rolled his eyes. "He can't. One-hundred-seventy-five people are the minimum needed to run the compound to its potential. Don't you remember your initiation? They need the people to do their jobs. That's why so many have been weeded out. If you dissent in any way, you're one of the first to go when new people come in. He wants followers."

"You seem to know an awful lot for a lowly guard." Dana chimed in, her opinion valid and welcome as my brain seemed to turn to mush under the onslaught of information and worry building about John and Bodey.

"Yeah, well," Mike shrugged. "Ethan talks a lot when we're scouting. Mostly creepy stuff about her." He pointed at me, curling his lip.

I had considered Ethan as an option for a split second, but realized quickly he wasn't the type of guy to be happy with something he caught once he captured it. He'd grow bored and toss me aside. Fortunately, I'd only let it be a possibility as a way to save Bodey and John, not as a possibility for my heart. Turning away from the choice hadn't been hard.

"Okay, so why is everyone in here? Why not just do what Rowan said and kill them?" I scrunched my eyebrows together. I would make sense of everything, if it killed me. Which, if I was honest, just might.

"Ethan can't kill anyone. He can shoot them to cause harm." Mike pointed at Captain Phahn and angled his eyebrow upward. "But he can't directly shoot anyone fatally. The fact irritates Rowan more than Ethan lets on. He brings them here and either lets them die or has a guard come take care of things."

We let that sink in, the utter finality in the offhand remark. One way or the other, the people in the cabin were always taken care of.

I licked my lips, my voice hoarse with nerves. "What will happen?"

Mike folded his fingers together and leaned his head back to stare at the dark ceiling. "We'll die. He doesn't bring food or water here. These guys were smart and collected the rain from the windows, but that food you brought in here will only prolong the inevitable. He won't come back. Not for a while."

I didn't remember it raining in that area, but that didn't mean it didn't happen. The mountains were fickle and weather changed fast.

"Why is Rowan having people killed instead of just turning them away?" I had to understand what was happening inside the camp. Like if I could understand the mind of the man leading things, I could guess his next step with Bodey. Understand which way he would go next. Desperation ruled me to estimate his next move.

Sighing, Mike shook his head, lowering it to meet my gaze. "A group came in and turned out to be bent on getting our resources rather than joining us. They asked more questions than they answered and they kept saying something about joining forces with someone else and taking over the rest of the area. When they mentioned revenge for rejecting them, Rowan shot them in the back as they walked out. He said he wouldn't sit around and wait for them to attack."

"Well, I wouldn't sound too upset about it, sure sounds like you would have shot them, too." I bit out angrily. Nothing made sense. My stomach twisted in confusion.

Shame colored Mike's face. "Actually, I can't shoot people. Curfew was set up and we're supposed to shoot people on sight, if they're out... and I can't. That's why Ethan brings me out here. I'm no good in there."

Dana made an understanding sound. "That's not a bad thing, to not want to kill people. Don't become like them."

Mike glanced quickly at her and then away. He peeked at me from the side of his eyes, pointing toward Simon. "We're never getting out of here. You should just let him die." He folded his arms across his knees and lowered his head to his forearms.

Maybe I should let Gary and Lance eat him.

CHAPTER 4

My back hurt so long, I don't remember not needing to rub the small indent when I just sat and tried to relax. What else was I going to do while waiting for something to happen?

The corner of the cabin offered support so I could slump to the side and sleep, if I needed to. I hadn't discovered the right way to sleep on a dirt floor yet, since being out of the camp. Something I used to do regularly before the return to showers and cleanliness. Would I ever find something steady and normal?

Dana approached me cautiously from the food pile I'd shared of Simon's. She twisted her fingers together and lowered herself beside me.

A phrase my mom used to say floated to my memory. I couldn't help but say it. "I won't bite." My voice even sounded like Mom's. I blinked back tears. She'd never meet her grandchild. I shoved the thought away, my emotional state worn and weary.

Dana cleared her throat and stared toward my stomach. "Did you say Bodey and John? Can I ask their last names?" Dana didn't mess with pleasantries or small talk. I appreciated the lack of preamble.

"Christianson. Yes, Bodey and John. My husband and my father-in-law." I smiled, but it didn't reach my eyes. Just saying their names brought a wave of longing over me. I didn't know what I was doing and I'd been captured by the one man I wanted nothing to do with.

Well, not the *only* man.

Ethan, Shane, and Rowan all held equal amounts of my animosity.

"Your husband and father-in-law?" Dana leaned her head back, tears suddenly streaking the thin layer of dirt on her cheeks. "My son and husband." She sniffed, wiping at her face. When she finally brought her gaze back to me, she smiled warmly. "So I guess that makes you my daughter-in-law." She tilted her head and reached for my hands.

John's wife. Shock reverberated through me. Oh my word, I'd found her. There she was and I wouldn't have found her, if we hadn't been captured.

Gratitude welled inside me. I gripped her fingers and leaned forward as much as my stomach would allow. "We searched and searched for you guys. Everywhere. That's all we'd done for the first sixteen months or so. We've been all over, following leads and following rumors." I glanced around, anxious to see her daughter. Hope renewed. "Where is..."

Wait, Dana was by herself. A shadow cast itself over our reunion.

Dana swallowed slowly. She looked away from me but held onto my hands, squeezing. "Jessica didn't... make it. We got to our house but found it burning. It couldn't have been set to flame long because the fire still moved around the pile." She pressed her lips together as if holding back a sob. "This last winter was hard. She, well, Jessica got sick and I think she had pneumonia and she... well, she didn't – she isn't around now. I've been moving around ever since."

"By yourself?" I didn't want to let her go. I had to maintain contact with her. Delivering her straight to John was all I could think about. He had to see her. He'd been without his wife for so long, he hadn't really smiled or laughed in a while. I gripped her arms. "Where did you go?"

Shrugging, Dana shook her head slightly. "Just around. I didn't care for a while. I figured Bodey and um, John, were dead. I wanted to be too, but I couldn't do it to myself. So, I just... existed." Sadness deepened the creases around her eyes.

I released her to rub at a tender spot on my stomach. "Yeah, I know." I recognized the feeling well. If Rowan succeeded in killing off my family, I wouldn't want to go on. I already felt more alone than I'd ever felt before – even since after my mom had died.

She cleared her throat, pulling her fingers back. Insecurity shadowed her eyes and she straightened her back, as if preparing for a hard truth. "Um, do you think John has forgotten me?"

"What? No way. You should see him. He's never happy and always has this distant look on his face, like he's lost something. The only reason we stopped looking for you is because these men chased us – had been since the bombings – and we'd run out of safe places to hide. So we made our way to Freedom Pass." I sighed, longing for our men overwhelming in the dark prison. "The frustrating thing is the men who had chased us joined the community not long ago, so even our supposedly safe place isn't safe anymore. Obviously minus the Rowan thing."

"That's my husband. Always taking care of his loved ones." She nodded, a wistful smile pulling at her lips. "Sometimes missing him so much overwhelms me."

"Me too. Him and Bodey. They've been my family since my mom..." I shrugged, the emotions so raw with Dana there, I didn't want to explore them too closely. "What do you think is happening inside? Do you think they're okay?" It wasn't fair to ask her opinion. She hadn't been inside, hadn't seen how things were, but ruminating with someone else helped, someone who loved them as much as I did, if not more.

"I wish I knew. This is all quite a shock. I'm so close but I can't get in?" She shook her head, the thick braid swaying behind her shoulders. "At least I got to meet you before I die." Dust lifted from the ground as she shifted on her rear to sit closer to me.

I softly slapped the top of her leg. "Oh, shh. We're not going to die. We can't." I wouldn't believe I'd come so far only to die in a pathetic hunting cabin. Outside fighting for my life? Okay, I would agree to a death of that caliber. But starving to death while imprisoned just wasn't how I wanted to go.

As if shaking off the pessimism, Dana blinked rapidly while twisting her head. She asked in a muted tone, "Tell me how you and Bodey met. How is he? I'm so happy one of my children is still alive." She wiped at the skin under her eyes again. She reached out and grabbed at my hand. "But first, tell me how far along you are? You look great. Are Bodey and John just ecstatic?"

Nodding, I bit my lip with emotion. Bodey would be so happy to see his mom again, to know she was okay. But his sister... He would be sad, but most likely relieved to finally know.

The not knowing about John and Bodey was killing me and it had only been seven days.

CHAPTER 5

The evening passed into night. Dana and I talked well past the time we should have tried sleeping. Eventually, though, we did find sleep as we slumped against each other in the corner of that dirty, woeful cabin.

My baby moved, kicking my stomach hard in the morning. Startled, I jerked away, cautious in my new surroundings. Everyone else still slept.

Simon seemed less restless as he reclined against two log sections we'd found abandoned by the wall next to the door.

Soft snoring came from Gary and Lance.

The guard had hugged himself into the corner where the floor met the door. He hadn't left his spot and I suspected he had some kind of weapon to protect himself, but I hadn't seen any sign of it yet. If I were him, I'd worry about getting killed in my sleep, too.

I needed to pee, bad, but I couldn't squat or stand in the corner like everyone else. The over-powering stench of urine and feces wafted around when a breeze broke through the small hole openings in the walls. The stench was almost vomit-inducing, except it reminded me we were alive. I found it hard to hate something which reminded me of that fact.

Talking with Dana about the men we both loved increased my sentiment that the Christianson family was one to adore. Where John was calm and solid, Dana seemed to have a streak of spunky fire evident in her laugh and the anger in her tone when we discussed Shane and Charlie. And Rowan.

Steadying myself on the log walls, I pushed from the ground to stand, trying to get above the stench and breathe in fresh air. I had to check on Captain Phahn – I mean, Simon. I'd never considered the fall of the world would also bring about so many lost identities. Twenty-two years in the service and he didn't consider himself a captain anymore. He didn't feel the authority was there to uphold his rating.

I felt differently. Bodey and I loved each other, our intentions were legitimate, and it wasn't our fault governing bodies had abandoned their duties. We were married, as far as we were concerned, and I resented anyone who would want to take that away.

Holding my urge to use the restroom, I tiptoed to Simon's side and knelt, careful not to nudge him with my knees. He'd held the socks to the wounds overnight. Only brown blood marked the material, not fresh red blood. This was encouraging and I claimed it as a small victory even as Simon's mouth hung slack, and his pale features worried me.

I shook his shoulder gently, careful not to scare him, but I had to know if he'd survived the night. Like a small part of my success as a person tied up in not losing him. I'd lost my mom because I'd been too young, too naïve and hadn't known anything. I still didn't know anything, didn't have access to anything which might help Simon, but I still couldn't help but feel like everything I was tied into his survival.

His eyes fluttered open, dark eyebrows drew together and he smacked his lips. Blinking at me, he slowly lifted his head. Awareness of his surroundings clicked into place as his features firmed with wakefulness. He stretched his neck and shoulders, then met my gaze, nodding briefly.

I whispered, to be sure I understood what he nodded at. "Are you okay? How do you feel?"

The strength of his gruff whisper tripled that of his voice the night before. "Still weak, but a lot better, thank you." He nodded again, his eyes piercing as he searched the room for information. I could almost see the captain in him striding back and forth as he called out orders.

"John said once you were up for Master Chief but you turned it down?" I'd enjoyed John's stories late at night with the stars in the sky above us. I'd always wondered why anyone would turn down advancement, especially such an autonomous one. "Isn't it a good thing to go up in rank?"

Simon met my gaze, a sad smile curving his lips. "In the Navy we don't go up in rank, we go up in rate. We don't do rank like the other branches. I wanted to do Master Chief, but I got in my own way. I was too hot-headed the summer I lost my wife to cancer. My senior office didn't recommend me and I didn't have the gumption to go up for the position again." He shrugged. "Captain is a great rate. It's comparable to Major in the other branches. I'm able to stay active as Captain. That's important. Or I *was* able to. Things change." He coughed, pressing his hand to his back. "Is there anything left to drink? My mouth is excessively dry."

I turned, grabbing up the last bottle half-filled with water and passed it to him. "Well, your life sounds interesting. The Navy sounds pretty amazing." The thought of so much organization astounded me. Why couldn't things have been in place to run smoothly where people knew their roles and they lived happily by them? Why did we have to trade who we were for a chance to just live?

He swallowed his swig and nodded toward the sleeping Mike. "Is he the only thing standing in the way of our escape?"

"Him and your injury." I wouldn't lie to Simon. He could handle the truth in all its grotesque and malformed glory. "You're not bleeding anymore, but I don't know how long that will last, especially if you're up moving around. I can't carry you and the other people in here don't have the energy to help you."

Simon nodded, looking away from me. He seemed to decide something, because in the next instant he shoved his hands on the ground behind him and pushed himself straighter, pulling his butt closer to the log rest. I withdrew my hands from his side, to give him space for whatever he was doing.

"You're going to reopen that wound, Simon. If you lose much more blood..." I couldn't choose for him, but moving so soon after initial healing had started wouldn't be the best thing he could do.

When he pulled his legs under him and moved to stand, I hurried to help and stood as well. Glancing around at the sleeping prisoners and guard, I whispered fiercely. "Simon, you're in no condition to be doing this."

"I'm not going to be the reason we don't do anything to get out of here." A thin white line formed around his tightly pressed lips. Creases etched themselves in his forehead and around his mouth and eyes. His pain couldn't have made itself more evident had he screamed from a megaphone into a full church of praying parishioners.

What was I supposed to do? He had to be aware that reopening the wound wouldn't be good. The potential for more bleeding was just that, possibility. There was no guarantee. I couldn't monitor him, if he didn't want to be watched. He was a grown man.

Dirt shaded the shoulders of his jacket and the lower part of his pants. Small needle fragments clung to his short hair and a smudge of dirt covered his upper cheekbone. I refused to consider what I looked like.

Nodding shortly, I moved to face him, careful to make sure I wasn't too far in case he fell. "But you were shot in your stomach." In my experience, he'd been shot in the worst place and the amount of blood testified to the dangerous area as well.

He shook his head. "Nah, it's just a side muscle shot. There's an exit wound. I'll be okay." Simon studied Mike, who hadn't moved with all the noise we were making, but whose eyes had opened. He watched our progress.

Limping toward Mike with his hand on the wall for support, Simon growled. The noise woke the rest of the occupants in the room as if bounced menacingly from the wood walls.

Mike sat up, bracing himself against the door with his hands tight to his chest.

Coming to a stop above the guard, Simon spoke clearly. "You're going to help us get out of here."

"Ha. Forget it." Mike shook his head. Simon leaned closer and Mike shrank into himself. Mike rushed to continue. "Hey, I don't want to be stuck in here, either. I'm saying, forget it because he won't be back for a long while. We'll be so weak by then, we'll want him to let us die or kill us."

"What about you? He won't come back early for you?" Dana spoke from where we'd slept. I tossed her a good-morning smile over my shoulder, but continued focusing on the men.

Mike arched his eyebrow at her question. "Seriously? He doesn't care about me. He wants to get rid of Rowan, Anyone who supports his dad, well, he doesn't really want around." His bitter laugh didn't quite make sense to me, but I let it go. I honestly didn't care much anyway. The tediousness of the whole thing grated on my hungry, tired, and aching nerves. "And why would he, right?"

Simon jerked his thumb in my direction. "Because we have her."

I looked around like I'd been caught stealing something. "Um, sorry?"

"You said Ethan is like a rabid dog about her, right? He won't be able to turn an obsession like that on or off. If he is obsessed, then he'll be here soon for her. When he comes back, which will be much sooner than you think, we'll be ready. And you're going to help us." Simon eyed Mike then glanced around at the two other men who nodded, their eyes bleary.

~~~

We were ready, pumped and primed, for the first hour or so. Then our energies lagged and the day passed painfully slow. I finally had to use the bathroom, which Dana held my arms for. Squatting didn't seem natural and my inner thighs hurt with the constant strain. Oh, how I missed my toilet at Freedom Pass.

The night came and went. Still no Ethan. For once, I started doubting his affections for me. I wasn't delusional in thinking he genuinely cared for me or even that I wanted him to, but the group relied on his feelings for me. Would I be letting them down, if he didn't show up? Like I wasn't delivering something that would help us.

While waiting, Simon didn't just sit there and ponder existence. He checked the walls for weaknesses and the holes for chinks or inconsistencies. He finally confirmed my suspicions that the openings were used to shove guns through. The cabin must have been someone's hunting blind.

How I wished a gun had been hidden or something, anything – even a butter knife would be welcomed at this point.

Our excitement over the plan to be ready waned.

The night passed. Our nerves had given up the fight hours before and I think we dozed in and out of sleep as hunger ate at us.

Staring at the holes sometime in the early morning, I couldn't help but notice the peachy cream of the sky. I blinked. Something in the air had changed. I cocked my head, blinking hard and fast. What had changed?

A humming seemed to vibrate beneath me, but not like an earthquake or even a train, it was just present, slightly noticeable. So slight, in fact, no one else stirred. I cradled my stomach in my hand and rolled to the side to stand.

Car doors clicked shut.

Suddenly alert, I spun, scuffing over the dirt to Simon and bending down to shake him awake. I whispered, "Simon, they're here. Come on!"

He jerked awake, bounding to his feet before he'd fully woken up. He winced, holding his hand to his side, but not before I caught a glimpse of shiny wetness on his dark shirt.

Standing beside the door, Simon crouched. I'm not sure if I held my breath or not – most likely since the stench from the corner hadn't lessened.

The door opened and Ethan stepped through, scanning the room until his gaze landed on me.

Simon pounced, thrumming his fist into Ethan's temple for the perfect shot to knock him out. Ethan crumpled to the ground, his head lolling when he landed.

"Thank you. I've been trying to figure out how to get him into a manageable position." Rowan stepped carefully into the cabin, fanning the gun in his hand from side to side to encompass us all. He prodded his son with his toe, but didn't look down.

Simon's shoulders drooped. He had to have expended the last of his energy on Ethan.

Rowan watched Simon. "Did you really think I would let him come back here alone? I'm not stupid or naïve about Kelly." He glanced at Mike. "You think I didn't notice the way you watched Kelly, too? For some reason she's like a dog in heat to you kids. She's nothing special. But you all wanted her." He shook his head. Staring at me, his eyes taking in all of my form, he scoffed. "I still can't believe I didn't see you were pregnant."

"Did you watch her, too?" Dana stepped up to stand beside me.

Rowan huffed, looking everywhere but at me, pink flooding his face. Then in less than a second, his face hardened. He drew back his fist and plowed a punch straight into Dana's cheek. I think that's where it landed. The thud sounded beside me as she fell, dropping like a bird shot from the sky.

I whirled back to Rowan. "Who do you think you are?"

He stepped close, his breath hot on my face. "I know who I am. I'm the leader. I choose who lives and dies. And now, I'm the one who's going to find out where your friend is from and then I'm going to go there and take every resource they have. I'll probably burn Freedom Pass to the ground when I leave, too." He shrugged, a glossy smile defining his enjoyment. "Who knows? I don't really care. Wherever I go, people tend to follow."

Rowan studied Simon, tilting his head. "So? What's it going to be? The location of your camp? Or do I shoot someone in this room?"

Simon didn't answer, just stared above Rowan's head with his jaw tight.

"No? Okay." Rowan lifted his gun, the barrel pointed at my forehead. He met my gaze, dark humor widening his pupils as they focused on me. With the barest shift, he turned the gun and shot over my shoulder.

I couldn't help it when I jumped. The sound cracked in the small cabin.

"Lance? Oh no, Lance." Gary sobbed with meager energy. Not a sound came from the shot man.

I didn't dare turn to check. Rowan was the kind of man who would kick me when I wasn't looking just to see which way I would fall.

Rowan returned his attention to Simon who hadn't shifted. He arched his eyebrow, jerking the barrel of the gun toward the ceiling. "Shall we go again? Where's your camp?"

Expressionless, Simon held his position, his hands behind his back, chest out with his chin up. He wasn't the kind of guy to remain unaffected by the effect of his actions. Simon was probably torn up on the inside that Lance had been shot. I understood where he came from, though. He had people to protect and Rowan wasn't going to get them as well – not for a couple people's lives.

Rowan didn't even look directly at Gary. He aimed from the corner of his eye and shot a few rounds to make sure he got him.

I jumped with each shot. Was I a coward? Everything happened so fast, I hadn't noticed if Dana moved on the ground. Hopefully, Rowan had knocked her out. If Simon didn't answer on this next one, Rowan would either shoot me or Dana. I couldn't fathom her getting this close to John and Bodey and never seeing them. It wasn't something that could be allowed by the universe. I would rather he shoot me.

Rowan lifted his gun and aimed at Dana, her stunned body still in the silence after the third shot.

Rowan arched his eyebrow at Simon who didn't look his way. "Do I have to ask?"

A heartbeat. A breath.

I slid in front of the barrel, closing my eyes as the metal dug into my shoulder and then collarbone. "Enough killing, Rowan." Opening my eyes, I stared at him, unflinching as he pressed the warm metal tube into my skin.

The light in his eyes promised he would have no trouble shooting me, if only to hear me scream.

BONNIE R. PAULSON

CHAPTER 6

Our challenge hung in the air.

"What are you doing? You think she matters? That you matter? You don't tell me what to do. The only value you have is what's growing in your stomach. And *she* can't have children. She's old." He laughed, not removing the gun from my chest. Each heave of his sarcastic chuckle shoved the weapon harder into the crevice beneath my collarbone.

Grinding my teeth, I narrowed my eyes. "She's not old, Rowan. Having babies isn't what defines us. We're people, not brood mares." I pushed back on the gun. *Either shoot me or lower the dumb thing, already.*

"Nothing defines her. She's expendable. As soon as you have that child, you will be, too." He lifted his jaw, his eyes half-lidded as he watched me.

I drew my hand to the side and then slammed it forwards, my backhanded slap landing squarely on his cheek. Shoving my hands by my side, I stood solidly planted, not backing down. "I'm not expendable. You're *nothing*. Your worth is in that gun, and nothing else. You think you're something because you kill people? *Please*."

Either his shocked reaction was to wrap his fist in my hair or he'd already been planning that because faster than I could register what happened, he coiled my dark locks around his palm and yanked me upward and close to him.

I bit my lip so hard on my gasp that I drew blood, the coppery taste bursting over my tongue.

"I'll show you my worth and just what this gun gets me." His husky words pressed into my cheek and the five-o-clock shadow on his jaw rubbed the soft skin beneath my ear like sandpaper. Stepping over his fallen son, Rowan dragged me out of the cabin, my feet bumping over Ethan's body and down the path to the Jeep.

Shoving me into the front seat, he leaned in, holding my head down while he spoke. "I'll shoot her first and then him, if you run. But they won't be kill shots. I'll make sure they suffer a long time." He squeezed my leg, ignoring my hands as I shoved at his fingers cramping my muscles.

I nodded jerkily, ashamed of my fear and my submission as he ripped his other fingers from the tangled mass of my hair.

Something I'd loved so much had been used against me. My pride had become my weakness.

He turned, striding quickly back to the cabin. When he reached the door, he didn't even look back to see if I'd obeyed his orders or not. Of course, he wouldn't look. His cockiness assured him I would be right where he'd demanded.

But I had to do something. I had to fight back, take away a weapon against me. He had lives at stake and I couldn't sit by while others were killed.

I didn't blame Simon. I understood why he did what he did, but I couldn't be idle while Rowan threatened others with my actions. I carefully opened the glove box and dug through its contents, glancing sporadically toward the cabin.

A standard first aid kit had been shoved to the bottom.

Hopeful, I pulled out the yellow box and lifted the lid. Everything was still in its original wrappings. Maybe I could use a scalpel or scissors to cut him, stab him. But there was no scalpel and the school issue scissors had blunt noses and plastic finger grips. My head hurt where he'd yanked on my hair.

Raising my hand to rub my scalp, I smirked at the glint on the metal lines of the scissors. I didn't have to think twice.

Chopping at chunks of my hair, as the long brown tresses fell onto my lap and the seat, I realized I'd never felt so liberated before. Faster and faster, but only as fast as the mediocre tool would allow. I'd go as short as I could, maybe look like a boy, then what value would I have? What weakness would he be able to exploit then?

The scissors dug into my skin in some places as I hacked and cut and chopped, sawing at hair I'd loved. Or rather, hair my husband had loved. An inkling of worry sowed inside me. What would he think when he saw me? But the Bodey I loved didn't care what I looked like. He'd be happy to see me.

I finally understood that my value to him didn't lie in my looks, but more in who I was.

Lowering the scissors as Rowan approached with Mike in tow, I stared ahead, taking a lesson from Simon on an impactful way to irritate Rowan. His footsteps slowed as they neared and then sped up.

He knocked Mike upside the head and yelled for him to get inside the car. Then he jerked open my door and grabbed at my hair, but the uneven too-short tufts defied his grasping. I didn't hold back my sneer.

Rowan's backhand didn't match mine in passion, but the strength in his surpassed mine. My head bounced off the seat rest and I clenched my teeth in pain. He ripped the scissors from my hand, scraping the skin from my knuckles. Rowan didn't say or do anything more. What else would he need? He spun and stomped back to the cabin, shouting something to Ethan who was slowly coming around in the doorway.

Ethan placed a hand to the side of his head. He swayed as he stood, clutching the door frame for support.

I was out of the cabin and I could breathe again – anything other than the scent of waste and body odor. The Jeep smelled like an old faded vanilla car freshener. With careful fingers I brushed my abandoned hair to the ground,

Inside, Rowan ducked down, swinging Dana up to his shoulder. He jerked his head my direction and Simon marched out the door, head up, pain tight in the lines of his face.

The Jeep wasn't large. We would be packed in tight. Somehow I didn't think this would bother Rowan at all. He didn't care about others, even when they were on his side.

Wending his way to the cabin on unsteady legs, Ethan blinked at me through the Window. then again, then faster until he picked up his pace, running at the Jeep while staring at my appearance.

He reached the door but didn't open it, studying my hair. Lifting a finger, Ethan traced my silhouette watching every line as if memorizing the way I looked. He clenched his jaw, finally meeting my eyes. He broke eye contact, looking to the side.

No matter what, I couldn't accept the blame in his gaze or the betrayal in the twist to his lips. Yet, a small piece of me feared Bodey would feel the same when he saw me. Would he feel differently about the way I looked?

Ethan stepped out of my line of sight, opening the back door and climbing in.

Once everyone was loaded, Dana in the back between Ethan and Mike and Simon sharing half my seat with me, Rowan turned the key and slammed the vehicle into gear. He didn't wait to see if any of us were steady as he spun the wheels. They grabbed for traction, lurching the Jeep forward.

We were in for a bumpy ride and I had to pee again.

~~~

As close as I was to Simon, I couldn't ignore the wet warmth soaking the side of my back where we touched. Every bump made us both wince. His wound hurt him and the baby didn't like the movement as the violent jostling shoved him or her up and down in my tight stomach.

Where Simon's arm pressed into mine, heat scorched my skin. I shot numerous glances his way, taking in the glassy eyes and the cracked lips. He hadn't had a fever an hour or so before. Hopefully, I was just being paranoid and over-exertion had caused the increase in body temperature. Such a fast onset couldn't be good.

Unfortunately, I didn't know enough about compresses or poultices to know off the top of my head what to do to help him. All I knew about was mint and gingerroot and their effects on nausea. With a nurse for a mother, I knew all kinds of stuff about modern medicine but we didn't have access to ibuprofen or codeine or even something as simple as aspirin. Some of the basics made all the difference.

The twists and turns of our drive didn't give away our position. I had no idea where we were headed and a part of me didn't care anymore. I was free from the cabin's stench and Dana and Simon weren't dead. So far, positives on my list.

How sad that a good thing for the day was not getting people killed?

Freedom Pass as our destination never occurred to me. At least not until we pulled up in front of the triple gates I'd left days before. How different things were when I approached willingly, then left with fear on my heels and now coming back as a prisoner.

Rowan waved at the guards in the towers and stopped the Jeep. "Ethan, I'm watching you." He unclicked his seatbelt and climbed from the driver's seat. Ethan followed suit and they switched spots before the gates opened. Rowan climbed in beside Dana, ignoring her altogether as he muttered. "Drive, son."

Ethan shifted into gear, avoiding my gaze. Dirt darkened his knuckles and he dusted the cuff of his jacket. Regardless of what he'd done and who he'd done it to, the fact that he was a puppet of his dad's couldn't have been more apparent in that moment.

And he knew it.

No wonder he was such a bully to everyone else. That and the fact that he had a few too many marbles jangling loose didn't help him look good.

The gates opened, all three in succession, and we drove through.

Very few people were in sight. A man walked alongside the inner gate, a guard walked behind him by a couple feet. I couldn't tell if he was under watch or being protected – from the bugs maybe? The only other visible person besides the guards on the towers was a woman taking clothing down from the laundry line closer to the kitchens. Another guard stood by her, bored as he tapped the butt of the rifle in his arms.

Ethan climbed from the car, affecting a swagger as he rounded the front. But he didn't open my door or even the one where Rowan had taken his seat. Instead, he flicked his hand at the closest guards and they approached the vehicle. Ethan stood off to one side, appearing distracted with his arms crossed and a foot out to the side. He watched us, but not extremely focused.

Our door opened and the guard roughly hauled Simon from his seat.

A shock of red hair made me catch my breath. *Please, don't let it be Shane.* I couldn't see clearly from my vantage point and when rough hands closed around my waist, I realized why coming back to Freedom Pass was the worst possible thing that could've happened.

I was back in the shark's cave, surrounded by the very predators I'd desperately wanted to escape. The ones I'd run from. The ones I'd left my family to.

Shane lowered me to the ground, making sure every inch of my front hit his front. I clenched my jaw at the obvious arousal in his pants. I stared over his shoulder, denying him the satisfaction of looking in his eyes. He roamed his hands up my arms and down my legs, pretending to do a pat down. His fingers lingered in the triangle of my legs and in the indent between my breasts and my stomach.

Ethan growled from behind me and Shane's eyes sparkled. He wrapped his hands around my upper waist and squeezed until I couldn't breathe comfortably. His husky whisper reached me just as spots dotted my vision. "You're lucky that spoiled brat is protecting you. Or you'd be mine." He winked and let me go, almost dropping me to the ground.

To give Ethan some credit when really he didn't deserve any, he rushed to my side and held my elbow. "Are you okay? That guy is crazy."

I shot a glance at Ethan's face. Was he serious? The saying 'takes one to know one' flashed in my mind. As this man's prisoner, I did the only thing left in my power to do. I drew on all my strength and spit as much saliva as I could gather into his face.

Recoiling in fear wasn't an option.

His fingers curled around my biceps and he dragged me from the parking area. Wiping his free hand down his face, he yanked me closer to him, ignoring each time I stumbled or tripped. We reached the clinic where I'd worked for so long and he pushed open the door, kicking my calf as I passed.

"Get in here. There's not a lot of damage you can do in here. After Dad strolls you around and people forget why they're upset, he'll finish the rest of you off. You will learn to respect me, Kelly. Or you'll die." Ethan's gaze promised more of his pain would transfer to me, if I didn't. "And you look like a boy." Like his insult would slay me.

I lifted my chin, tormented by the need to defend myself but also to protect my baby and the people I cared about. Would he push me further? Do more than toss insults at me like live grenades?

"Nah, she doesn't look too bad." Shane winked, shoving Simon inside beside me and unceremoniously deposited Dana on a medical counter. Her hand flopped to the side. He winked as he walked by me, ignoring Ethan's glare.

Crap, I'd done something that appealed to Shane. Why couldn't I do anything right?

They left and I turned to Simon. "Are you okay? We need to check out Dana and see where Bodey and John are." But what if Dana didn't survive after so long? She'd been tapped pretty good and her features had paled considerably.

After the door clicked shut and the lock ground into place, Dana sat up, pushing at her hair and smiling at Simon and me. A dark red blemish promised a bruise would show up soon on her face.

"You were faking?" I moved to stand beside her, taking her hand in mine. Her cheekbone didn't look too swollen but that wasn't always a good thing. If her bone underneath were broken, swelling might not show up until the next day.

She wrinkled her nose, squeezing my fingers. "Only in the truck. I came to when he was carrying me, but didn't want him to know. You okay?" She glanced between Simon and me and then over my shoulder.

Her body froze and she gasped, her fingers coming to her lips. The padding of a boot on the floor sent the hair up on my arms.

Fear coiled in my stomach. What now?

CHAPTER 7

I turned my head enough to catch a glimpse of what she saw.

Shifting to the side, I allowed gratitude to well inside me as John and Bodey approached Dana in slow motion. Simon moved to join me, give the family some privacy.

But I couldn't make myself go far. This was my family now, too, and I hadn't seen my husband in a long time – well long enough for me.

Long enough to imagine every single possible torture and death scenario.

Long enough that my heart hurt from the distance.

Long enough to regret leaving.

John stared at Dana, his eyes light above thick dark and silver stubble. He walked like pushing through air made of gel. He didn't stop, his hand reached out to her, tears bright as they fell down his cheeks.

Dana held out her hand, waiting for him. She didn't speak. Barely breathed as her husband walked toward her.

Their fingers touched, intertwined, until John wrapped her in his arms and their lips melded together. Dana sobbed as they kissed, breaking the connection to enclose him completely in her arms. They moved so close together I couldn't tell where one ended and the other began. Their shoulders moved with softly silent crying.

Over Dana's shoulder, John's face was just barely in view. His lips were pulled back, baring his teeth and his eyes were squeezed shut. Tears poured down his cheeks, disappearing into the hair on his face.

Was it joy? Was it sorrow? I couldn't pinpoint their emotions, only that my own heart hurt watching their reunion.

Bodey slid up next to me, never taking his eyes off his mom. His hand engulfed mine and he tucked me in front of him, carefully feeling all of me as if to search me for injury. He nuzzled my neck, beneath the chunky ends of my horrible haircut. Regret tasted bitter and I waited for him to push me away in disgust – maybe I had been too impulsive. With him right there, touching me, I didn't want to have made a bad decision. I didn't want to push something deeper between us.

"What happened to your hair? What did they do to you? Are you okay?" His stilted murmurs didn't spread around to anyone else. I tried to turn around to talk to him face to face, but his steel-like hold refused my efforts.

That's right. We'd been fighting when I'd left. I'd pretty much abandoned him. I couldn't imagine what he thought about me. I hadn't wanted to allow myself to dwell on it too much since I'd left because I would go insane with the what-ifs and the regret. Yet I had – both gone crazy and overthought everything.

Choked up at the situation and that I couldn't read his face for his reaction, I squeezed his fingers and pointed at his parents. His mom hadn't seen him in so long.

He returned the squeeze. But still he waited, giving his mom and dad their reunion time. And us ours.

Dana and John parted enough for space, but they leaned their heads together. Foreheads touching, eyes closed, they held onto each other's shoulders to continue the connection.

Simon moved to sit down on a cot beside a window. He swung his legs up and lay down, careful to turn away from our small family gathering.

John's whisperings reached Bodey and me. "Where's Jessica? Where have you been? I've been searching, I... I couldn't find you. Where have you been? Dana... I..." His tears started fresh, as he softly shook his head – not enough to break away from his wife, but enough to assuage the surge of emotions overcoming his body.

"She... Jessie, well, she didn't make it. I... tried everything, but it was... unavoidable at that point." Dana's ragged answer split the joy from the reunion.

Bodey's shoulders slumped forward and he stared at the ground, tears in his eyes. I couldn't move as I watched the last of their hope stream away.

"Who killed her? What happened?" A storm of pain-filled rage shadowed John's face. His knuckles whitened as he waited for Dana's answer.

Dana cleared her throat. "She died of pneumonia last winter. I couldn't get us warm enough, no matter where we went. Not enough food. She..." Dana didn't continue, just shook her head and pulled back from her husband, wiping her face and looking to the side.

Lifting his hands, John framed her face. "Stop. You didn't do this." He ignored her shaking her head and he tilted her chin up. "Look at me, Dana." He waited but she stared off to the side. Quietly, he repeated his order. "Look at me, Dee."

She lifted her eyes to his, self-hate stark in her gaze.

"You couldn't stop it. You're a terrific mom and you did everything you could. Stop blaming yourself. Stop. Do you hear me?" John's tremulous smile warred with the tears coursing down his cheeks. "I didn't lose Bodey, but that was the grace of God. Jessica's not hungry anymore. She's not cold. She's not lost in this forsaken world anymore. She's safe." He gripped Dana forward into a tight hug, rocking with her.

Motioning Bodey forward, John drew back enough to wipe his wife's cheeks. "Here, now. Your son missed you, too."

Dana raised her tear-soaked face to Bodey's and sobbed. "Bodey, oh son, I…" She fell into his arms, her face on his shoulder and his arms enveloping her. Dana held out her arm to her husband and they created a cluster of familial love and longing and loss.

Tears formed in my own eyes and I couldn't stop them as they freed themselves, marking paths down my cheeks.

"Where's Kelly?" John lifted his head from their embrace, finding me and motioning me to join them. "Come on. Dana, you met Kelly? This is our newest addition to the family. She and… Jessica were friends." He choked on his daughter's name, grief strong in the jerky motion of his head.

Their arms pulled me in and we folded together, rocking and swaying in gratitude, love, happiness, and sadness. What a mess of emotions and I couldn't handle them in my pregnant hormonal state. I sobbed, desperate not to create more chaos, but I missed my own mom, more than anything. We seemed to go from celebrating to memorializing our loved ones and our situation in moments, while welding ourselves together as a family unit.

Right then, I became a Christianson more than when I married Bodey and more than when John had taken me on almost two years ago. With Dana's acceptance, I'd gone from one piece of the family's growth to an important member of their group.

"We found each other, guys, we found each other." John's murmurs cascaded around us and we enjoyed the reunion for a while longer.

My hope rose. We could do anything.

Even save the world.

CHAPTER 8

We broke apart after our group hug cemented our bonds.

John held Dana's hand and wouldn't let go. He turned toward Simon who had turned to his uninjured side, forcing him to face the wall.

As terrible a medic it made me, I'd forgotten about Simon and his injury. Releasing Bodey's hand, I rushed to Simon's side. "I'm so sorry, Simon. Can I stitch you up?" The thought brought my old friend, nausea, to the forefront, but I swallowed the roiling queasiness back. I could survive a lot of things. I'd be hanged before I'd allow a little blood to do me in. Last time that had happened, I'd lost my mom.

Loss was not something I was going to welcome anytime soon.

I reached for Simon's shoulder and helped him sit up. Heat emanated from him in waves. To Bodey, I murmured, "Can you get me some cool damp rags, please?" He nodded and slipped away. He'd find them, if he didn't already know where they were.

The last time I'd dealt with a wound like Simon's… *Don't focus on the past, just get him taken care of.* I shoved my memories and regrets to the background. I didn't have any magic herbs or medicines. All I had was alcohol, soap, sewing thread and hopefully a steady hand.

"Do you think you can move to the counter over there, Simon?" I needed him responsive. The worst thing I could think of would be him dying while I sewed or just plain dying. Period.

His weak nod alerted me to his previous adrenaline overload. He was down and failing fast. How badly had he overextended himself for the sake of pride and survival around Rowan? I motioned to John, who hovered nervously nearby, to grab Simon under the other arm and help me move him where I needed him to go.

"I think you need some water and maybe something to eat. What do you think, Simon?" Turning my head, I glanced at John under Simon's chin. "Have they been feeding you in here?"

John nodded, avoiding my eyes. "Yes. Every evening meal we've had a ration to split. It hasn't been terrible. There are some snacks hidden in the back in a box, too. We haven't been to work, so we've been a little bored, but overall, things haven't been awful."

"The guard said you were screaming when Rowan visited?" How could things have been okay, if they'd been screaming? Men like John and Bodey didn't tend to scream for no reason.

Abashedly, John rubbed at the back of his neck for a minute before answering. "Well, I honestly didn't think you'd find out." He pressed his lips together and didn't comment further. Who had screamed and why wouldn't he say anything more? How bad had it been? I searched Bodey and John's appearances for signs of any physical pain.

Simon walked grayly to the counter and struggled to get on top. I chewed on my lower lip, watching.

Dana was the first to notice I hadn't moved closer to Simon and seemed incapable of moving. "Kelly, are you alright?" She closed the distance between us and placed her hand on my shoulder.

John reached out and offered Simon his hand to help his friend to the counter.

I scrunched my nose. "Yeah, I'm fine. I just… I don't have any anesthetic for Simon and, the stitches are going to hurt." My hands shook and I hid them behind my back. I had to hold my calmness together because stitching someone up wasn't trivial like sewing a patch on jeans.

I'd be calmer, if it was.

"He's going to be fine. Just do what needs to be done. We're here to help." She gave me a reassuring hug and gently pushed me toward the clinic shelves. They hadn't been restocked since I left and the minimal supplies worried me. Inventory was kept tightly controlled by Ethan and Rowan in the hangar and since I hadn't been there to order things, no one had refilled items.

Moving the lessened supply of alcohol, cotton pads, gauze squares, butterfly needles, catheters, oxygen masks, and surgical tape, I searched for stitching supplies. Cammie had always pulled what looked like a small traveling sewing kit out of a drawer. She'd snapped gloves on and then…

Wait. I could do the same thing I'd seen her perform over and over. Or try anyway.

Crossing my fingers, I rushed to the drawer beside Simon's limp legs. Inside, a small rectangular kit had been tucked into the corner with a box of gloves and some alcohol pads. I snapped on the gloves, the sound reminiscent of Cammie. I almost looked around to see if she was there. I hadn't had to perform any stitches when I'd manned the clinic for the short time after Cammie was killed. I hadn't been asked to do much that would require experience.

The kit was light. Deceptively light. Hopefully, it wasn't empty. How disheartening would that be to get that far and have nothing in there? I rolled my shoulders and stretched my neck to either side, nerves made me want to run and hide in the closet.

"Kelly, I'm okay. I'm just tired." Simon struggled to keep a pleasant expression on his face, but pain and fatigue warred for a hold and his eyes closed and then opened, closed and then opened – not in a blink, but more like an attempt to sleep but he kept waking himself up.

In about two minutes, he wouldn't have any problem staying awake.

John moved closer to Simon, trying to fill Simon's space with his presence. "Do you have any idea what to do, Captain?"

I refrained from pointing out Simon's belief on his rate. I didn't want to bring more attention back to me when John might be able to distract Simon somewhat.

Simon grimaced, focusing on a spot somewhere close to my ear. His eyes had a glazed appearance like he tried to be anywhere other than there. Maybe he could take me with him.

A stack of gauze pads would clean his wounds nicely. "Can you lie down, please? I need to clean the wounds first."

He shifted carefully to the side, and I helped him come to rest on the cot. Simon breathed in sharply. Yeah, that was only the beginning. I patted his shoulder in reassurance. "You're okay. We'll get started once you're ready."

Simon nodded, swallowing roughly. "Thanks." He stared at the ceiling. "Did you find out where they get their electricity? Like a generator or something?"

I lifted his shirt hem from the waistband where he'd tucked it. The material had stiffened as the blood dried and stuck the shirt to his skin. Dribbling some water from a cup onto the shirt to loosen the blood, I waited a moment and then narrowed my eyes and slowly tugged it free. Hair or maybe even scabbing had been connected to the shirt because he winced when it broke free. I didn't have time to wait for it to soften completely and neither did he. I breathed easier that there wasn't any sign of pus.

"The process isn't something I quite understand. There's a man here who is the lead electrician and engineer. Rowan keeps him fairly sequestered, but one of the mechanics is a cousin or something – Paul Blakely. From what I understand, the system is self-sustaining and easily repeatable." John had moved to Simon's side and spoke to him in his direct line of sight, so Simon wouldn't have to move his head.

But Simon continued staring at the ceiling. He blinked, as if processing what John said. "What's the general consensus from people? Are they all with Rowan? Are they against him? How much help do we have to fight here?"

I rolled his shirt up and tucked the crusty piece under his armpit, using the weight of his arm to hold the shirt in place. Dabbing gauze on the lip of the alcohol bottle, I took a deep breath. "Simon, I'm applying the alcohol to clean around the wound. I'm sorry, this *is* going to sting." I didn't have anything else to clean with or I would use something – anything else.

He hissed when the cold pad touched his skin, the abrasions stretching minutely where I couldn't see the fine lines. I hurried. No reason to take my time torturing him. But at least I was doing my best to prevent infections, some small amount of relief in that.

John rushed to answer Simon's question. "Actually, many of the people here don't like the way Rowan runs things. But willing to fight with us?" He shook his head. "I'm afraid we're looking at only about seven or eight families. Not many."

But seven or eight were more than zero. Families could be anywhere from two to however many people Rowan let in as a group. The numbers could add up significantly.

I wiped an alcohol pad on the needle and the length of the thread I would use. His wound in the back had jagged edges and I wasn't excited to work on that part. But the front had a nice clean hole. The edges would be easy to draw together and might only need three or four tight sutures. The rear exit wound would need considerably more.

Procrastinating on the first poke, I tied a knot in the end of the thread and wiped the curved needle once more. Cammie had said pushing hard was the only way to get a needle through the skin.

"Seven or eight sounds better than two." Simon smiled tightly as if he knew what was coming.

I cleared my throat. "Simon, I'm going to do the first stitch on the front wound, okay? Please, try to breathe normally." Or was it hold his breath?

Panic welled inside me. What if I didn't do it right and he died from my treatment? That was the opposite of what I actually wanted to happen by helping him.

I glanced up, catching Bodey's gaze and smiling nervously his way. He nodded slowly, a smile warming the air between us. I couldn't tell if he was still mad at me or not, but his encouragement meant more than I could let on at the moment. Ignoring my own advice, I inhaled deep and held my breath.

The tip didn't slip through the skin like I expected. I jerked back at Simon's gasp. What was I doing? I couldn't do it. Cammie had said it could be hard to give stitches, she'd never said anything about fighting through something as durable as shoe leather.

Bright red blood on the fingertips of my gloves brought memories of my mom's death to mind. I'd stopped helping her, scared, unable or even unwilling to face my fears because I didn't know what would happen.

But I knew now. If I didn't try my best, I would for sure lose Simon. Not trying was the same as giving up. Even if I lost him after I tried, at least I could look back and say I did something. That hadn't been the case with Mom. That was a regret I'd carry the rest of my life.

I gritted my teeth. "Okay, Simon, sorry about that. Let's get this over with, okay? I'm shooting for four or five on this side. Ready? Here we go." I didn't wait for an answer. What would he say? No, wait, I need something to eat first?

My fingers gripped the needle with more assuredness and I breathed out as I pushed the needle through the tough skin and layers of fat. He wasn't a heavy man, but everyone had fat on their abdomen and fat tissue wasn't soft or malleable.

Ignoring his flinch and gasp, I tied off the first stitch. "Next one, here we go." The second one went smoother and by the time I got to the fourth stitch, I was faster and more certain.

The veins in Simon's wrists and hands stood out in stark relief with the intensity of his hold on the side of the bed.

Tying the last knot, I leaned back and nodded at John. "All I need to do to the front is bandage it. Good job, Captain Phahn."

His hands released and his body visibly sank further onto the cot with relief. He closed his eyes. He'd never survive stitches on the back. I might not be able to do them anyway with the massive torn edges. He wouldn't survive, if I didn't do them though either.

Simon breathed deeply, in through his nose and out through his mouth. Finally, he slowed and glanced at John. "I think we need to try to get the people together and overthrow everyone on Rowan's side."

"With what? No one has guns but the guards." John shook his head and crossed his arms.

I wiped my tools down with alcohol and yanked off my gloves. Speaking offhandedly, I tossed the garbage into the burn box. "Too bad we can't get into the armory. Rowan has more guns in there than anything, from what I understand."

No one answered me and I glanced up to find everyone staring at me.

"What?" I turned back and taped the gauze squares with surgical tape.

"There's an armory? How do you know that?" John leaned forward as if I had all the secrets to the end of the world.

I leaned back because I didn't. "The guard... he said that his one gun was nothing compared to how many guns Rowan has. Remember, Simon? Dana? You were there." I shrugged. Did it matter? "Rowan has it under the inventory warehouse in the hangar. You'll never get in. He has it protected." Plus, how would they get out of the clinic to get in the hangar?

Simon shook his head. "I don't remember that. I was pretty out of it and just barely holding things together when I was standing." He shifted his hips. "It doesn't matter if we have a thousand guns and a million rounds of ammunition, if we don't have the support of the people."

Bodey stared at a spot on the bed. "Too many people are afraid of not having something to eat or not being protected from what's out there. I remember when we got here Rowan promised we would get our guns back at some point and we never did. I bet no one else has weapons allowed to them."

"Yeah, you're right. The mechanics are fed up with Rowan's crap though. I could get the graveyard shift to get involved and get into the armory. We would have enough people to get somewhere with this, if we had a few weapons other than wrenches and shovels." John braced his arms on the side of the cot. "We would have roughly twelve men to fight initially."

"I know some guards who would turn, if they knew they had options." Bodey leaned toward the men, engaged and frightening as I pictured him involved in a shootout or something with bullets zinging around him.

"Sounds terrific, guys, but how can you do any of that when we're trapped in here?" Dana pointed toward the doors. She glanced at me. Like we'd known each other for years, I understood the lift of her one eyebrow meant she didn't think the guys were thinking clearly.

"Well, Bodey and I found a secret way in and out of the clinic. There's a garbage room with an incinerator. The room has an emergency back door access. A sign says an alarm will sound, if it's opened, but we opened it and no alarm sounded. The door opens to the garbage area and no one can see that spot from the towers." John wrapped his arm around his wife. "But it's a valid point, Dee."

"Could we use the exit to get out? Escape all of Freedom Pass?" I was anxious to get out of there, get away from Rowan and Ethan and their crazy, obsessive ways. I arranged the items around me to work on Simon's exit wound.

John nodded slowly, but glanced at Simon while he spoke. "Too many people who aren't on Rowan's side – don't deserve to die – plus, there's no other way out of the perimeter fencing. Those front gates you strolled out of haven't been added to. If anything, the guards have doubled."

I'd noticed the increase in guards when we'd driven up. Rowan didn't want anyone out or anyone in. I couldn't fathom the need for that kind of control. I grinned. "I hadn't really strolled out, you know. That was so scary. I ran as fast as I could."

Should I worry more? Did we want to break free from food and relative safety? As long as Ethan and Rowan were around, Shane wasn't going to touch me. I could live with that for a little while longer – even if Rowan *had* said that he was going to finish us all off. Yes, I sounded cowardly, but I didn't care about anything else when the safety of my baby was threatened. I needed a break from running and being scared.

"You ran? With the baby? Are you okay?" Bodey pulled me close, his concern warming me. If only he knew what I'd done while pregnant, he'd be so much more worried about us.

BONNIE R. PAULSON

CHAPTER 9

To cover my concerns I nodded. "Yes, with the baby." I laughed. "Did you think I could take the baby off and run?" He chuckled and I playfully punched him. I wanted to hug him and hold him, but things still felt off. Did he not want me? Was that why he'd pushed me toward Ethan? I only considered Rowan's option because of Bodey's fast suggestion that I'd take it.

John grinned at Bodey and I, then spoke to Simon. "What about Bayview? How do we warn them about Rowan?"

"As soon as we get out, I'll head that way and warn my group. It would be in both camps' best interests to immobilize Rowan somehow." Simon grimaced as he stretched his side. To me, he added, "Is it supposed to hurt after you've stitched it?"

"Sorry, I don't have pain medicine or anything. I can only offer you a cool pad or something to put on it." I stood, moving to the freezer. One nice thing about having a camp with electricity – ice and ice packs were in abundance upon demand.

"I'm surprised we're not being supervised or something. You would think in our position we'd at least be separated or something." I pulled one of the last ice packs from the top tray and wrapped it in a smooth white towel before placing it on his bandaged area.

John spoke up, watching as I administered to Simon. "They don't have enough guards to watch us and all the rest of the people who may or may not revolt. They put us in here – at least according to Rowan – because it was the only place in the compound that he could watch from his quarters, if he wanted. I think they just don't know what to do with us. Anything could cause more problems."

"So this is like a desperate dungeon?" I couldn't help voicing my concern. "I know this sounds naïve, but do you think it will work?" Had we been imprisoned in the medic clinic because Rowan hadn't prepared for a revolution? Was he really so cocky to believe that his rules and laws would go unchallenged?

"Will what work?" John shifted his gaze to me.

I shrugged, threading the next needle. "All of this. What's the point? I mean, what are we trying to accomplish? We have electricity, food, warmth, a roof. We even have medical supplies. Is it so bad here?" I pushed at the air in the direction of the rest of the camp. "I mean, besides the craziness, of course. Isn't this what we would want to settle down in?"

Fear mounted in my chest, welling with each word and breath. Where would we go that I could have my baby in safety? Rowan wasn't safe, but we could do something about him, couldn't we?

Simon and John glanced at each other, but Dana saved them from having to call me a stupid girl or something else, not that they would, but I could sense that's what they all wanted to say. Or maybe I was being paranoid. Either way, I'd just come back from eating strictly rhubarb and I didn't want to go back. Not after eating mashed potatoes and fried chicken occasionally.

Dana cleared her throat. "Kelly, that makes sense what you're asking. Actually, I can see the appeal of turning my head away and ignoring what Rowan does. Food, warmth? You bet, especially after losing Jessica." Her voice trailed off and she cast her eyes downward.

"This is where our earlier conversation comes into play, Kelly." Simon's pinched expression opposed the gentle understanding of his tone. "All of this comes down to the worth of a soul – any soul. Your soul, my soul, even Rowan's soul."

"Right. I understand." Warmth filled my chest. I did understand. I finally got it and things clicked into place. Hopefully one day I could tell my mom that my soul wasn't worth a piece of chicken and some mashed vegetables. I was going to hold out, be grateful I had been given rhubarb, and stop complaining.

But we could do it. We would be safe as long as we were together. Calming warmth covered me. The safety would come from us being together. I could handle the rest.

Simon and John spoke strategy and Bodey pushed his way closer to me, rounding the counter and closing his fingers around my elbow. Tingles covered my skin where we touched. "Can we talk, Kel?"

I nodded, but only because my tongue felt like it had swollen to the size of a cow's tongue and chills ran up and down my back at his touch. I'd missed him. He could have whatever he wanted. I didn't even want to remember what we fought about.

Tucked into a small corner where Cammie had stored garbage bags and cleaning materials, Bodey pulled my hands into his. "I'm sorry I volunteered you to go with Ethan. I didn't want you to go to him, but I don't want you to die even more than that. Ethan has access to so much more than I do. He could make sure you're comfortable. All I can promise you is that you will at least have access to evergreens and dirt."

"Stop." I pushed on his hands, peering up into his strong, newly-a-man face. "I've lived on rhubarb this last week, rhubarb and water. No toilets, nothing. And while I missed food and bathrooms, I wanted you more than anything. I can deal with less than nothing as long as I have you." I screwed my lips to the side. "Is that dumb?" Why couldn't I be secure with my decisions? Everything I said or did lately I second guessed.

"If it is, then I'm there with you. I feel the same way. I had everything this week, except I was in here, and I would trade it all to have you back. I promise to make sure that never happens again." He bent his neck and touched our foreheads together. Rubbing the tip of his nose to mine, back and forth, he closed his eyes. "Don't leave me again, though, okay? For anything. We'll figure it out. That's my baby, too, and I love you too much to lose you. I can't…" He choked on his words, hiding his emotion behind a small cough. "Yeah?"

"Yeah." My answer was soft and breathy. I'd missed him more than I could reply anyway. I loved him – probably more than was healthy, but I couldn't help it. Something in me needed him to survive. And recognizing that made me stronger. Hopefully, we would figure out a way to settle somewhere together.

I'd hate to lose him to someone as twisted as Rowan or Shane.

Honestly, I'd hate to lose Bodey. Period.

CHAPTER 10

We waited for the cover of night.

A knock on the door and a grating of key in the lock warned us about the meal arriving. Who would bring it? Who would we see?

We all rested on separate cots, waiting. I'd moved mine closer to Bodey's and John and Dana had tucked theirs closer together behind shelves.

A dark haired woman kept her eyes down as she entered and placed the small tray of food on the further counter from us. She left faster than she'd entered. Could she have been a potential ally or was Rowan only feeding them so that he wouldn't look bad?

The arrival of the meatloaf and baked potatoes almost brought out the animal in me. Gravy, onions, corn, potatoes with margarine. I couldn't stop myself as I shoveled my portion in my mouth.

In between bites, I shot an apologetic glance at Bodey and John. I hated not having manners, but even Dana hastily shoved food in her mouth. We'd been too long without sustenance. I'm not sure how much longer the baby could go. Bodey smiled sweetly and pushed the rest of his small servings my way. And I didn't turn it down. He was feeding the baby, too, and if I rejected his efforts, I was just punishing our little one.

I leaned toward him and kissed his lips in gratitude.

After the gnawing ache in my stomach subsided, replaced quickly with an overtight sensation, I lowered my fork and sipped my water. "So let me make sure I have this right." I pointed at John, Simon, and then Bodey in succession as I spoke. "John is going to the mechanics' shop to speak with the graveyard shift and see about access to the weapons underground. Bodey is going to see what guards he can bring to our side – which isn't very safe considering they have guns and everyone knows he's supposed to be locked up." But I lifted my eyebrow and continued. "Simon is scouting out the perimeter for an escape route and keeping an eye out for Rowan, Shane, and Ethan."

"Right." The men, led by John, nodded their heads, their mouths in various stages of eating – except for Bodey who drank his water.

I tapped my finger on the makeshift dinner table. "What I don't understand is why Dana and I are staying here? I'm not worthless and Dana has proven herself to be more than capable of surviving on her own." I drew my eyebrows together, searching the men's faces for answers.

John shrugged. "I can see how that would be annoying, but I'm not concerned enough with your feelings right now." He held up his hand at Dana's spluttering. "I know, honey, I know. But you and Kelly are worth too much to Bodey and I to put you in further danger than you need to be. I won't be able to focus while I'm worried about you two." He redirected his attention and pointed at my stomach. "Excuse me, three."

He slammed our arguments with the mention of the baby and that his or her safety would be in jeopardy. I hated when they did that. John continued, "And anyway, we need as many supplies as possible packed and ready to go when we get back. If you do that here while we're gone, it would save us more time and energy in the long run."

We were packing, Dana and I. Which was fine, but for what? For who? For when? We might not even leave until the next day or the day after. The men were more or less going scouting tonight.

"Remember, if anyone shows up and tries to get information about what we're doing or where we are, ask for the passcode – pineapple. This is anyone but us. If they show up, don't even talk to them without the passcode, alright?" Simon's color had returned and held his hand to the rear wound that I'd stitched up. Thankfully we had some oversized clear post-surgery bandages that hold things in.

"Are you sure you're going to be okay?" I wasn't certain he should be going outside, but he insisted on doing a perimeter check, probably to loosen his muscles up and walk the pain out a little bit.

He grimaced, attempting a smile. "It's just a small flesh wound. I'll be fine. Thank you." Simon focused on the task at hand. "Small flesh wound" wouldn't be the term I used to describe a two-inch jagged hole. I hoped he was okay, but there was nothing more I could do.

"I'll be back. Stay safe, okay? I love you." Bodey pulled me into his arms and grazed my lips with his. His piercing blue gaze warmed me.

I returned his kiss, our energy melting into the other and mixing, rejuvenating. "I love you, too."

John, Simon, and Bodey tread quietly down the hallway toward the burn room. Dana turned away, not able to watch, but I watched every excruciating step. What if I never saw him alive again? If Rowan captured them sneaking around, trying to stage a coup, he'd trap them and then set up something public to use them as an example.

Bodey's blond hair disappeared behind the door and I allowed myself to breathe.

I sat up on the edge of a counter, rolling my head back on my shoulders and gusting out a poof of air. Kicking my feet into a soft swing, I glanced at Dana. "Now what?"

She offered a slight shrug. "Now, we wait."

BONNIE R. PAULSON

CHAPTER 11

Pacing up and down the slight aisles bugged me more than just sitting still. Finally, I gave into the urge to use the toilet and rushed in, pulling my pants down even before I closed the door. Sitting on the seat, I glanced at my underwear, the sight of bright red spots freezing me in fear.

As soon as I finished, I exited the bathroom, afraid that so much was slipping out of my control. "Dana, can I ask you a question?"

"Of course." Dana pulled items from drawers, placing them on counters and grouping them with like items. She glanced at me, spying the seriousness of my mood. "What's the matter?"

"I'm spotting. Does that mean the baby is coming?" I couldn't contain my fear that I was going to lose the baby. I was way too early. If the baby came then, he or she wouldn't make it. We had some first aid supplies and I could fake my experience with a cut or even a fever, but I didn't have a breathing machine for the child or anything. "I don't even have diapers or clothes to put the baby in."

Panic set in and I gasped for breath. Closing my eyes, I braced my hands on the counter, panting. What was happening to me? Why couldn't I get this under control?

Arms wrapped around me, tightening without being painful. Dana shushed me softly, turning me toward her. She pulled my head to her shoulder and rocked me. "You're okay, Kelly, just breathe." She swayed with me as I calmed, the ache inside my chest dimming. She pulled back enough to see my face and ducked to see me fully. "You're spotting? Any cramps or anything?"

I shook my head. "Could there have been cramps? I'd assumed my stomach pain was because of hunger. What if I'm losing the baby and I've been so focused on eating, I wasn't paying attention?"

She shook her head, stroking my arm. "You're okay, I spotted all the time with my pregnancies. It's perfectly normal. Just keep an eye on it, alright? Especially the further along you get. You said you're just past six months, that's about the right time for spotting." She directed me toward the cots where Bodey and I had sat. "Let's relax for a little bit. Maybe try to sleep while the men are gone."

"Don't we need to pack?" I didn't resist her suggestion. Lying down on my side sounded like the perfect idea. I curled my arms around my stomach.

Dana scrunched her nose. "Nah, we'll have plenty of time to pack everything we want, after we sleep for a little bit." She held my hand, her fingers warm and soft – like my mom's used to be.

I'm embarrassed to admit I pretended Mom held my hand and spoke to me as I drifted off to sleep.

~~~

A rough hand over my mouth woke me, cutting off my breathing with the side of their fingers pressed against my nose.

My eyes snapped open and I clutched at the arm across my chest, clawing for air, for release. Staring up into Ethan's eyes, I tried shaking my head, twisting and turning to get him free of me. Dawn light ate the shadows, displaying the stark, empty room to my frantic gaze.

Where was Dana? What was happening?

He shoved his face close to mine, alcohol staining his breath as it heated my cheek, ear, and neck. "You…" Rearing back and pulling his hand from my face, he thrust his forefinger into the air directly in front of my face. "You don't get to throw me away. I know you love me, you want me. Why wouldn't you?" His bloodshot eyes couldn't seem to focus and he wavered on his feet. I could've used that alcohol while working on Simon, figures Ethan had to go and make himself crazier.

I lifted my head, looking around for Dana. Where was she? But she was gone – no, wait, she wasn't.

The bathroom door opened and Dana stepped from the opening, her eyes growing wide. "Hey, what are you doing? Get off her." She ran to me, intent on saving me from Ethan's hands.

He laughed, shoving at her when she got close enough. "Sit down. This doesn't involve you." To me, he pointed and offered me his hand. "Stand up. I have so much to prove to you."

A muffled grunt pulled my attention toward the door. I sat up, ignoring his hand. "What is that?"

Ethan shrugged. "Not what, who. My father. The great Rowan. Want to see?" He didn't shake or even stutter, but waited for me to stand and then guided me toward the front of the clinic, his hand on my lower back. His touch sent creepy chills through my gut.

I swallowed. A shiver chased down my limbs.

Where was Rowan? No one waited in the front. The only people in sight were me, Dana, and Ethan with his manic hand waving.

No, wait. There on the floor. I gasped. Rowan had been trussed up, his feet bound and hands tied behind his back. I stopped. *Oh my word, what was going on?*

Ethan pushed his way around me to kneel beside Rowan. He pulled a knife from a sheath at his waist. "See, Kelly? I'm not weak. I'm not weaker than him. He's just a man, just like everyone else here." Ethan tapped the torn edge of tape he'd covered Rowan's mouth with. The man on the ground glared at me, unable to turn his head toward his son to deliver a scathing stare.

Glancing at me, Ethan narrowed his eyes in desperation. "See? I'm not weak. I don't do what he wants. He's never happy with me. I'm perfect but only as long as I do what he wants. He wants me to shoot and kill people and I just don't do that. I don't like guns." He twirled the knife in his fingers, the skill with which he handled the metal both graceful and terrifying. "But I can make you both happy. I'll prove to you I'm not weak and he'll finally see it also."

Confused, I glanced at Dana as she moved up beside me. I drew my lower lip between my teeth and turned my attention back to Ethan.

He groaned. "I love when you do that." He pointed at my mouth. I quickly released my lip. I would probably never do it again after hearing that.

Ethan ripped the tape off his dad's mouth.

Rowan growled. "You're pathetic. I've given you everything and you tie me up? Are you joking? When I'm out of this, you're going to get it." He twisted his head to see Ethan. "Get over here where I can see you, you piece of crap." Anger marred Rowan's normally pristine calm. To see the men without perfection surrounding them, turned my reality upside down.

If Rowan couldn't control Ethan, then Rowan wasn't all-powerful. The rest of the compound needed to see that. The ability to turn people to our side would be immeasurable.

Ethan laughed. "I love when your true feelings coming out, *Dad*. Makes me certain I'm doing the right thing." He looked up at me, his face earnest. "Kelly, we'll be rid of him. You and me. And then we can go wherever you want, or stay here, anything. You'll stay with me, won't you?" Like desperate for something he wasn't sure about. Could be a mommy complex.

"She's not going to stay with you. She's common. You're my son. We could rule this area. Lead it to greatness. And you're going to throw away the chance because of her? She's *common*." Red flooded Rowan's face. He strained his body, the ties holding against his attempts to struggle free. Where was Rowan getting the holier-than-thou attitude? Were they royalty or something? I'd never heard of them before everything fell.

He stopped, panting, and then he turned his eyes toward Ethan, lowering his voice into a conspiratorial murmur. "Look, rape her, cut parts off her body, do whatever you want. Go over in the corner and do anything you'd like. I'll help you get rid of her afterwards. But you're not going to throw away everything I built for this community because she won't let you screw her. Do you understand? I've worked too hard to leave you something with value for you to trade it in for…" His eyes shifted toward me and he spit the words. "That."

Dana reached forward and claimed my hands in hers. She patted my clenched fingers softly. Even her attempts to comfort me didn't work.

"Come on, Dad." Ethan grabbed Rowan by his ankles and dragged him out the door on his stomach, over the threshold and onto the patio outside the front door. The clinic wasn't a bunker but was on ground level within easy eyesight of most of the compound.

Leaving Rowan on the cement slab, Ethan returned for me, wrapping his arm around my waist and leading me forward. "Oh, Kelly, we'll be so happy together. Just do what I ask, be what I want, and I'll give you anything you desire. You'll let me then, right?"

"Why do you want me so bad? I'm nobody. I'm nothing. There are so many women here who are interested." Incredulous, I held out my hands and slowly followed him. I honestly couldn't figure his obsession out. "Come on, Ethan, be honest. I'm not gorgeous. I'm pregnant with another man's baby, for crying out loud. What is so dang appealing?"

He stopped, looking down at my stomach, my feet, then at my face. "It's like I get whatever I want so nothing seems important, but then I can't have you, no matter what I do or my dad does – nothing. I… I realize I'm going to have to finally work for something – somebody – and that must mean you're worth it. My mom fought my dad on everything. And he never replaced her because she was matchless. He couldn't replace her. You're just like her." He glanced at Rowan. "I can keep Mom… I mean *you* and I'll be better than him."

Sadness shadowed his features, like he had to do this, had to keep his mom alive with him somehow.

The truth about just how bad he'd lost his grip on reality was staggering. If I didn't say something just right or I did something that would make him mad, he could lose it. The danger intensified as I realized he was a grenade without a pin and could go off with or without encouragement. As much as I hated him, I reached out and touched his arm. "I can't promise you anything, Ethan." I swallowed, biting my lip for him – hoping to distract him. "But wow, look at how low you've brought your dad. What an amazing accomplishment. You should share what you did with all of Freedom Pass. Let everyone see how strong you are. You've definitely impressed me. Maybe one day, you'll tell me more about your mom." I shook my head and smiled softly to add to my lies. He was close to snapping but I didn't want it toward me. "You don't have to do anything to prove yourself, you know?"

He lurched away from me. "I knew it. We'll be so happy together. Once *he's* gone. Don't worry. I'll show you. I'll show everyone!" He spun from me, opening his arms wide and shouting to the encampment. "Freedom Pass! Want to see what you've been hoping for? Come see the great Rowan taken down." He dropped his chin to his chest and held his arms aloft in a Y-shape. "Come out! Come out now!" His voice carried, slipping and sliding over the rounded tops of the bunkers, reaching further and farther with each syllable.

Doors slowly opened in bunkers and over by the hangar. People emerged from their homes, rubbing at eyes and wrapping jackets tight over their chests. I hadn't realized how chilly the weather had gotten. All my focus was on Rowan and Ethan and the spectacle they created. Hopefully, John and Bodey could utilize the distraction.

Hopefully Bodey didn't find out what I'd said.

Rowan had fallen eerily silent. He stared at the crowd, searching, seeking. He stilled and arched his back when his gaze landed on someone. "Shane! Get this lunatic out of the way, untie me."

I shot a look around the crowd, spying Shane on the edge of the crowd about twenty feet away at the same time Ethan did.

Rushing forward, Ethan cut the ties holding his dad's feet immobile and yanked Rowan to his feet. Rowan pulled and pushed, trying to run from Ethan. Thrusting his knife forward, Ethan controlled Rowan with the rope around his wrists. "Don't come closer. I'm doing this."

Shane didn't move, just watched from the edge of the crowd as people gathered in a loose semi-circle around us. He flicked his stare in my direction, taking in my form from head to foot. Dread slithered everywhere his eyes did. When our eyes met, he nodded ever so slightly, the angle of his lips menacing and promising all at once.

Shoving Rowan to his knees, Ethan grabbed Rowan's forehead and slammed his head backwards. Rowan shifted, shuffled, staring up at his son. "Don't do this, son. We're family. We need each other."

I pressed my fingers to my lips, a small whimper escaping through my teeth.

Glancing at me because of the sound, Ethan nodded carefully. "This will fix everything." He returned his gaze to his dad and spoke clearly. "You think I'm weak? I can't kill anyone? I can't take charge?"

Rowan swallowed, sweat breaking out of his brow and temples. "No, please. Ethan, don't do this. I'm your father."

"Yep, and I'm going to make you proud." Ethan plunged the knife in a sweeping motion across the base of Rowan's neck, yanking the blade toward him. No remorse. No guilt. Just relief and satisfaction settling his features.

A red shower of blood sprayed outward. Rowan gurgled, then his eyes stared upward and Ethan released his head.

The body slumped to the ground, blood pooling where it landed.

I shuddered, relieved Rowan was gone, but the emotion was short-lived because Ethan and Shane hadn't disappeared. And as horrible as Rowan was, he at least kept Shane off me.

Ethan turned toward me. I took a step backward. The crowd of people watched as he smiled, hand outstretched as if to hold mine. Why wasn't anyone doing anything?

A loud bang and a red hole appeared in Ethan's chest.

Screams from around the clearing punctuated the air.

Ethan clutched at the immediately saturated area about where his heart would be, fear and shock twisting his lips and widening his eyes. "Wha—"

Falling to his knees, Ethan stared up at my face like I'd done it. Like I had shot him without a gun. He fell the way of his dad, arms mingling with his dad's legs.

I raised my eyes, searching out the shooter. My gaze lit on Shane and he strode toward me, rifle raised in his hand. Fear filled me, all encompassing. No more barriers between him and I. Glancing around at the group, he inclined his head. "Freedom Pass is now mine. Gather together what you want to take with you because you're getting out."

The residents within earshot gasped.

"Now." He didn't yell, but his voice demanded immediate action. People dispersed, bumping into each other as they tried to leave quickly.

What about me? What about Dana? Why wasn't anyone helping us?

Backing up, I gripped Dana's hands. "Where are the guys, Dana? We need to get out of here. Now."

Every step Shane took brought him closer to me – his target.

I shook my head, backing into the doorway. The unrelenting doorframe bit into my spine.

Things couldn't have gotten worse than if Satan himself showed up.

CHAPTER 12

Shane approached, his confident stride drawing him inexorably closer.

Every muscle tightened in my body, freezing my progress as I tried to move back, escape. Dana tugged on my arm, pulling until my joints creaked. But I couldn't move.

He and I had been on a collision course since day one and everything came down to right then, right now.

Shane took the steps two at a time. He stopped in front of me, his eyes bright and his smile fierce. "Hello, Kelly. Aren't you going to run?"

"Where would I go?" But oh, I wanted to run. I wanted to fly. I don't think I'd ever wanted anything more than I wanted to escape that situation in that precise moment.

He reached out for my arm and I flinched, but his touch was gentle, caressing almost as he turned me toward the door.

My gaze flew to Dana. She watched in anger as I moved with him. Maybe she was mad at me. I wasn't fighting or struggling. What would happen if I did? He would probably like it more, make me hurt more.

I didn't want anything to hurt more than I knew it was going to. Shane was sick and he'd only like my pain more.

Dana shoved at Shane's chest as we passed. But it was like he'd expected it. He grabbed her arm and jerked her in front of us. His strength was obvious. "Can't have you running around trying to get in the middle. Let's do something with you, before I get started on my time with Kelly." He leaned down, nuzzling my cheek, his auburn whiskers scratchy and rough. "I feel like I've been waiting for this forever." He chuckled. I shrank inward, rubbing my belly with my free hand to comfort both the baby and myself. Things had gone from worse to worst when I missed Ethan.

Shane kicked the door shut and threw Dana toward a chair – one of the swivel stools anchored to the ground. He pointed at me, his eyes narrowed. "Go pick out your bed and wait beside it. Please, run, I want you to." He winked. "I'll even give you a head start."

Run? I wasn't in any shape to run and if he wanted me to, I wouldn't do anything that would bring him joy.

Dana sat stoically, watching him, as if waiting for something interesting. Shane yanked rope from his back pocket and twisted and tied the length of orange twine around Dana.

I desperately struggled not to run while his back was turned. My flight instinct strong while carrying my baby.

He finished with Dana, her eyes murderous as he turned from her and slowly ambled around the counters, trailing his fingers over the black surfaces. He watched me, a feral hunger in his eyes.

A deep chill overtook my limbs. My instinct carried over to my baby and he or she kicked and fought, as if it too could feel the danger stalking us.

"Sit down, Kelly." His husky voice grated like a saw on rough bark.

Glancing at Dana, I bit back my pride and slowly lowered myself to the cot I'd positioned next to Bodey's to sleep. The men hadn't returned and if they were smart, they would stay away. Shane wasn't dumb and he had to have his own henchmen. They'd be watching the front door, protecting Shane from anyone or anything that might interrupt his revenge.

He didn't reach me for a long drawn out minute. When he did, I had to lean my head back to see him fully. My face was at his pelvic level and his grin suggested he'd already considered the implications.

Shane's glance at my chopped hair filled with derision. "What a shame you had to cut your hair, Kelly. I would've loved to grip that and rip it, chunk by chunk, from your head." He smiled while speaking, like he wasn't discussing harming me in horrible ways but instead offered me compliments that I would blush at.

"Well, Rowan wanted the same thing, so it's gone." I smirked at him, my smugness a cover for the thick blanket of fear working itself up my legs, my hips, and my abdomen, to my chest to constrict tighter and tighter around my ribs.

Shane didn't acknowledge my comment. He pushed at my shoulder until I lay down. He picked my legs up and straightened them out on the cot, arranging me like an oversized doll.

I folded my hands over my stomach, severely uncomfortable. What was he going to do?

From a pocket in his cargo pants he pulled out a different ball of twine, and unwound a length from the orange mass. "You know, I didn't always focus on one girl like this. Charlie taught me the fun in chasing after someone specific and then capturing someone else. You can make the substitute do whatever you want while pretending they're the one you're really after." He grinned, his disarming charm so silky even as he withdrew a shiny knife whose blade had a sinister curve to the tip. "It draws out the real moment a long time."

How many women had he hurt because he wanted the same sick fun as Charlie? How many women had Charlie hurt? Guilt and worry and sadness swamped me and I started coughing at the pressure on my chest.

"Whoa, whoa. You're okay. Breathe." Placing the knife on the counter above my feet, he stroked my hair and rolled me to my side to pat my back.

Alarmed at his seemingly twisted sense of humor, I watched him with widened eyes when he rolled me back to my flat position. He carefully drew one of my hands up to anchor to the metal corner post of the cot, tying it with a length of the rope he'd cut from the ball.

Again, so slow and considerate, he did the same with the other arm, touching me with butter-smooth delicacy. I didn't trust him for his soft ways and his caring touch. Not when he whispered to me as he touched me. "I can't wait to cut you. And make you bleed. There's a certain spot on everyone where, if you nick it just right, they don't stop bleeding. I wonder where yours is." He smiled, his teeth white like a shark's. "I hope I don't find it for a while."

After he had me tied to the cot, testing the twine with multiple tugs to ensure each knot was tight, Shane stood and removed all of his clothing – except his tight brief-style underwear.

I turned my face to the side. He would rape me. In front of my husband's mother. With my husband's baby in my belly. I avoided looking at Dana. I didn't need to add embarrassment to my list of traits at the moment.

He retrieved the knife from the counter and twirled the shiny blade back and forth in his fingers. "Do you know what a six-month old fetus looks like?" Shane knelt on the ground to the side of the cot. "I don't. But I have a feeling I'm about to find out." He finished the last of his words with a sing-song tone.

Dana jerked forward on the chair, the squeak as it moved loud in the silent clinic.

Shane didn't glance her way or give her any attention. He'd tied her pretty well, she wasn't going anywhere.

If he cut my baby out of me, then I would die too. My child and I would be together with my mom and dad and brother. I wouldn't give anything of myself I didn't want to take with me. He couldn't have the parts of me I'd given to Bodey. Shane would just get the carcass of my body.

Not my soul.

I stared at the ceiling as he slit the knife into the neck of my shirt and sliced the material from my torso. I controlled my breathing, careful not to jar myself and accidentally get cut before he wanted me to bleed. As long as he was gentle, I would take it without screaming. I hoped.

No matter how prepared I thought I was, I wouldn't be able to handle the pain of being filleted. Hopefully, I didn't scream too loud.

My stomach boldly protruded into the air, like the bow of a ship. My son or daughter had no idea they would soon be ripped roughly from their warm home and killed. I had no emotion. Like a sudden calm had enveloped me.

Shane watched my face, but not a tear fell. I wouldn't cry. I couldn't. Like part of my soul wouldn't allow it. He couldn't take my pride from me. Well, he could, but not without a fight.

I stared at him, steely control maintaining everything from my breathing to my heart rate.

His pleasant expression didn't change as he drew the curved tip of his knife softly along the line where my stomach bulged from my abdomen, where the baby's pouch connected to me.

He pushed the tip in slightly. I flinched at the burning sensation as he sliced me so softly, not deep but like he traced the curve of my stomach. Down around the low waist of my pants and back up under my breasts. Finally, the pain became unbearable and tears coursed down my cheeks. I stared at the ceiling, my hands in tight fists and straining against the ropes. My shoulders ached from the tension.

"I didn't think you'd be a bleeder so soon." He shook his head, disappointed in the hot blood seeping from my skin.

Did I tell him my mom had always been anemic around her period and I had followed in her footsteps? Did I tell him at school blood drives, I'd been turned away multiple times because of the thin state of my blood? Did I tell him, I hoped he drowned in my blood?

I didn't say anything, just clenched my teeth, even as a whimper worked its way up my throat.

He bit the blade of his knife and held it between his teeth while he unbuttoned my pants, trying to yank them down my hips. His hands slid from the blood and he fell backwards, the clang of his knife on the cement floor loud as it echoed from the clinic walls. "Sonuva—"

Looking at Dana wasn't an option. I couldn't even console my body as it stung and bled. How did I help it when I couldn't press my hands to the wounds? I rolled to my side, trying to put the sheets against the cut to help stop the bleeding.

A shuffling of boots on hard flooring drew my gaze. Was he coming back to do more damage?

Shane hadn't stood and was in fact surrounded by a group of men led by John and Bodey. Simon stood off to the side, cutting Dana's hands free from the chair. Another man rushed to my side, a pair of industrial scissors in his hand.

Bodey's jaw tensed as he took in my condition. He didn't wait to find out any details or see what John wanted to do with Shane. He bent over and wrapped his arms under Shane's chin and squeezed. Shane struggled, but Bodey hadn't been starving or lazy the last year and a half.

His strength was that of a young man and his anger added the power of two more men to his corded arms as he stretched Shane's neck.

My attacker's face reddened then turned a harsh shade of purple. His eyes bulged and it sounded like his teeth popped.

The man with the scissors cut at my ankles and my wrists, careful to avoid looking at me. I appreciated his manners while in my vulnerable state. When my hands were freed, I rubbed at my chafed wrists and covered myself with the remaining scraps of my shirt.

John tapped Bodey's shoulder. "That's enough, son. We'll get him taken care of."

Bodey shook his head as if waking from a haze. He reluctantly released Shane who slumped to the floor at their feet, semi-naked. My husband rushed to me, pulling at the remaining twine. "Kelly, oh no. Are you okay?"

My arms wrapped around him and sobs I didn't know I'd been holding burst forth. My stomach hurt, burned, and I didn't know if the baby was still secure with all the blood I was losing.

Grabbing a sheet from his nearby cot, Bodey pressed its length to the stinging cuts and swung me into his arms. He sat on a chair with me cuddled on his lap, pulled tight to his chest.

The hum of the men talking reached me as I snuggled my face into Bodey's neck.

Dana's voice came through clearly. "Rowan and Ethan are dead."

"Yeah, we need to get out of here. We saw everything as we came around to the back. There are so many people out there fighting now, since Shane came inside. We need to go." John's voice broke through the confusing collection of men they'd brought with them into the clinic.

"My family is still in the bunker." One man's fear started a string of panic to rip through the small group.

"So's mine." Another man spoke.

"Mine, too." And yet another different voice I didn't recognize.

"Gather your families and get to the hangar. Hold on tight to your guns, people are going to try to take them." Simon's calm leadership acted like a balm to the chaotic group and the hum slowly died as they stopped murmuring to listen. "I know this is scary and a lot is going on fast, but if we can get everyone ready and out of here fast, it will be easier to leave. The longer we wait, the harder it will be to survive this."

I slid my face up to peek over Bodey's shoulder. One of the men watched from a window by the door. Shapes and shadows rushed past.

"Go out the back and meet at the hangar. Grab all of your things. Remember the passcode." Simon clapped each man on the shoulder, one at a time as they passed him.

After each man had left out the back, he approached John, stepping around Shane's unconscious body. Pointing down at Shane, Simon asked, "What do we do with him?"

"Obviously he dies. Kelly, how do you want to deal with Shane? This should be your decision." John carefully turned Bodey on the swiveling chair to face him, Simon, and Dana. I turned my head to watch them, and to keep Shane in my line of sight.

Bodey's body tensed more, which I wasn't sure was possible. Something warred within him.

I didn't want to see anger on his face but I needed to know he wasn't mad at me. I peeked at his expression and drew a sharp breath. Even mad, Bodey wore his emotion tempered with concern. But it wasn't his decision. It was mine. "I want him dead." I spoke with a deadpan tone, as if there was no other answer. And there wasn't. Not in a sane world. Not in my world.

My husband squeezed me softly and met my gaze before speaking. "I want him dead, too, but I don't want to deal with him. I don't want to kill anyone. And as your husband, I can't ask anyone else to do this for us." His voice broke on the last word and he lifted his gaze to his father. "I'm not sure what the right answer here is, Dad."

John folded his arms. "I agree taking care of him would be the smartest answer. If we don't, I fear he won't stop. Even if he doesn't come after Kelly anymore, it doesn't mean he won't harm others." He nodded at both of us.

Dana watched John and Bodey. She stood back a few feet, not in their line of sight. She arched her eyebrow as they discussed Shane's fate. Calmly, she moved closer to where Shane had fallen and she picked up the knife he'd dropped. Without any fanfare or warning, she stepped over Shane's sprawling legs, bent over his chest and swiftly sliced his throat.

His body jerked and then was still.

"Done." Dana dropped the knife beside Shane's inert body and stood, moving to claim her position beside John.

Bodey half-stood with me in his arms as he watched Shane bleed out. He and John turned their eyes toward Dana, staring at her in disbelief.

She ignored them, smiling at me as if she'd just bought me a fur coat for Christmas and couldn't wait to see me open it.

John wrapped his arm around Dana's shoulders. "Dana, you should've let us deal with him. You don't want that kind of blood on your hands."

She twisted her lips into a semblance of a smile. "I have worse stains on my hands than killing the man who'd tried raping and killing my daughter-in-law and taking my grandchild from me." She looked intently at each one of us in turn. "Can we go now?"

Relief infused me and I tried to stand. Taking a breath, I forced myself to inspect the cut. One long cut circled my stomach, but it wasn't deep. The knife had penetrated just barely past the first layer or so of skin – enough to bleed but not to be permanently damaging.

It hurt like it was going to rip off.

Dana left John's hold and knelt beside me. "Let's wrap the sheet around you like a big bandage. I'm sure we can get more clothing, if we need to, where we're going." And she opened and then folded the sheet into a large bandage, securing the length around my stomach and over my bra. She tucked the ends in before pulling my jacket on over it.

"Grab anything you want to keep. Did you pack the medical supplies from here?" John retrieved a wheelchair from the back storage room and opened its folding frame beside me. "Here, Kelly, this will make things go faster."

I slipped from Bodey's arms into the seat, embarrassed I needed it, but grateful at the same time. Shane's death relieved me. But with his dead body so close by, something inside me was disturbed. Yes, it was either him or me, but when was that going to stop being the norm?

"Yes, I packed everything into those duffel bags on the end table." Dana pointed at four bags I didn't see her pack. John and Bodey each claimed two and Dana moved into position behind me.

"We'll go out the front, but watch yourselves. There are desperate people out there. I'm not sure how far they will go to keep the resources here." John waited until we all had positioned ourselves in front of the door before swinging it open and allowing the screams and yells inside the clinic.

Was it bad I wanted to close the door and hide?

CHAPTER 13

People ran in all directions.

A fight had broken out along the end of the clinic between four or five men. I couldn't tell what it was about and I didn't want to hang around to find out.

Dana pushed the wheelchair down the slight ramp and onto the gravel path. "Which way are we going, John?" Every bump and rock ratcheted the wheelchair like it climbed through mountainous terrain.

John pointed toward the large hangar about a hundred yards north of us. "There. One of the men is securing the vehicles."

Vehicles? We were going in cars? I never saw enough cars to get everyone out that had just been in the clinic with us. All those men and their families. "How many do we need to get out?" I couldn't remember the number because I'd been so focused on Shane and Bodey. The men's faces had blurred together.

"There's only about thirty of us. We found Paul Blakely. He's waiting in the shop with his brother." John ducked as he pushed us forward. "Go fast, Dana, Bodey stay on Kelly's other side."

Each bump wasn't easy to traverse with the thin wheels of the chair. We lurched to a stop three times, going so slow. I stood. "Enough. Thank you, but come on." I didn't need to be wheeled. The throbbing pain around my stomach was just that, pain. I could handle it. Judging by the fact that my baby was still intact and no organs spilled around my feet, I wasn't going to fall apart either.

A man appeared as if out of nowhere, grabbing my shoulder and yanking me toward a bunker. We hadn't made it more than fifty feet from the clinic. I couldn't be sure who he was as he had me from behind. The cold steel of a gun barrel pressed against my neck. "Give me your bags! Anything you have on you. Now!"

Anger split Bodey's anxious expression and he jumped on the man, toppling them both to the ground. A bang retorted and I jumped. Bodey climbed from the body and held the gun out by his waist. His face was tight and in that second, he aged a decade. His eyes focused on me and he looked me over. "Are you alright?"

I nodded, taking his hand when he neared me. Tucked close to his side, I speed-walked with him to the barn. I ignored the abrasive material of the sheet as it rubbed my tender cuts with each movement. Okay, I didn't ignore it very well.

We cut the distance to the hangar fast and pushed our way in through the large doors on the shop end. I'd never been allowed inside that cavernous portion of the building.

Oversized tires leaned against one wall while a collection of five or six rolling toolboxes manned the opposite wall. Large enough to house eight varying vehicle types, the garage offered Jeeps to trucks with covered beds.

A young man with overalls on passed out keys to each vehicle. "You only have five people in your party, John. Do you think you can make do with a truck? We're out of Jeeps."

John glanced at us, as if calculating in his head. "Yes, but I'm going to load it up."

The man grinned. "Of course. We left the door open to the warehouse." He pointed to the side where women and a few men rushed in and out with their arms filled with packages. "You better get going though, the convoy is about ready and the remaining residents are already ransacking the place."

I gripped Bodey's arm. "I know where everything is. I can get us stuff fast." People darted in and out of the opening. We needed to be quick about what we were going to get.

Bodey looked to his dad, resignation in his clenched jaw. "We'll be right back."

John nodded and turned to Dana.

But we left before we could hear what she said. Pushing our way through the doors, Bodey reared back at the chaos inside the normally calm warehouse. "Kelly, stick close. I don't want anything else happening to you." He didn't know I wasn't leaving his side for anything.

I tugged him toward the water bottles. Ethan had stored them by the lanterns and bedding on the last shelf under the stairs. Pulling Bodey's arm, I walked on tiptoe to whisper in his ear. "I stashed MREs behind the extra sheets." I'd been bored one day and watching Ethan stress about incorrect numbers had colored my mundane time with him.

On the end of the supplies shelves, mobile supplies like backpacks and bedrolls filled closets.

A couple pushed past us, arms laden with bottles of ketchup and vinegar. The woman glanced back at me, mouthing sorry, then turned down the aisle filled with jelly and chili.

Bodey and I didn't stand around waiting. We pushed forward, heading to the water bottles. The rate of people entering and exiting the warehouse was dizzying. We would most likely only have time for one trip.

The closet on the aisle we wanted hadn't been touched. Flares, First Aid kits, towels, pillows, and flint stocked the top shelf. Bodey grabbed a folded duffel bag from the bottom cubby and shoved everything from the top two shelves that would fit.

Three more bags had been placed neatly in the same cubby. Taking all three, I turned the corner into the empty aisle. My step faltered. Why was the aisle empty? Had I missed something? But the stairs could've thrown people off, leading them to believe nothing was stored that way. Or maybe they just hadn't made it into the building that far.

The storage under the stairs transferred easily into our bags. Bodey dragged three behind him on the floor, one filled with bottled water.

"Wait." There had to be an easier way. I pointed toward another closet secreted behind the open bathroom doors. "Ethan…" I gagged on his name. "He kept a dolly in there."

Bodey closed the door and wheeled the blue handcart down our aisle. Stacking the bags, he claimed my hand and pushed the lot of items toward the door.

A few aisles down from us, closer to the door, a woman screamed, then a gun went off with a pop.

Bodey picked up the pace. A flash flood of panicked people crowded around us, dropping items in their rush to escape. Growling, Bodey shoved us ahead of them, getting us through the door and back into the garage.

"I thought we were all supposed to be working together." I gasped, grabbing tight to his solid arm.

Looking around for his parents, Bodey shook his head. "Our people are already loaded. These are residents who don't want to leave." He pointed his free hand toward the over-sized garage door opening. "There. Come on."

We broke into a half-jog as more people than I'd ever seen in Freedom Pass at any given time surrounded us, pushing and struggling to get into the warehouse for resources.

No one really worked on the vehicles. They hadn't thought that far ahead yet. What they wanted control of seemed to be the food and supplies.

Maybe Shane's death hadn't registered yet. Maybe they thought he would come out and take over again. Rowan's strict rationing could have spurred gluttony in anyone. While I complained about the rhubarb, a positive had been that I could eat as much as I wanted or had near me. No one divvied out just *one* serving at a time.

Feet from the truck, Dana stepped from the cab and helped us swing the bags into the back, her on one end and me on the other while Bodey loaded two on his own. She reclaimed the front seat and Bodey helped me up into the bed of the truck to sit beside Simon, our backs against the part by the rear window.

A few vehicles had already started the crawl out through the crowd. People surged around the cars, like ants around a leaf.

John revved the engine and we fell in behind a Jeep with five more people in it. Packed around Simon, Bodey, and I, boxes of tools and medical supplies as well as toilet paper – thank you! – and gardening tools had been haphazardly stacked.

The crowd seemed to realize all at once we were leaving, escaping with supplies, and they weren't. Almost as one, the collection of people turned toward us, slapping their hands on the sides of the trucks, grasping for a handhold to get out. Desperation hung in the air as their cries strained over the hum of the engines. Screams and yells filled the air.

I gripped Bodey's hand in mine.

A bump and a scream sent my face into his Bodey's shoulder. John shifted and we picked up speed, plowing through those people who tried to stop us with their bodies.

All three gates stood open, no longer protected by any guard as each ran amongst people fighting for survival again. How many wouldn't make it since being softened by Freedom Pass?

The throng of people thinned and shrank as we pulled out onto the gravel road leading away from Freedom Pass. Cool air brushed my cheek and I realized I hadn't thought of the cuts on my abdomen in a little while – at least not in the excitement of escaping the triple gates of a place named for freedom.

Simon pressed on his shoulder, grimacing as he watched the scenery pass. The wind ruffled his collar and whipped the few strands of hair that I'd missed into my face.

"How's your side, Simon?" I called over the shouting wind and the engine roar.

He shrugged the opposite shoulder from the one he grabbed. "The pain's dimmer there than in my shoulder." He pulled his hand away, his palm bright red and shiny.

"Oh no. You're shot again?" The man had to be a magnet for bullets.

Simon nodded. "The shot in my side made it hard to run. There are more people back there with guns than I thought." He winced, returning his hand to his wound. "I'm sure it's not a big deal. We'll get to Bayview and I'll see if they can do something for me." But he didn't look convinced, like somehow the double shot had scared something into him he wasn't prepared to deal with.

I wasn't prepared to deal with him getting shot. Again.

Smiling, hoping to brighten his mood, I asked, "Did you notice there aren't any children in our group? Or anywhere? I might have the youngest baby around. That's sure to get some special treatment." I winked, ignoring the sinking feeling as blood seeped between his fingers.

He grinned. "Actually, there are quite a few babies in Bayview – well, okay, only three, but you won't be alone." He tilted his head, tired bags under his eyes. "But I'll be sure to spoil your baby." If he made it that long. True uncertainty that he wouldn't filled me, bringing goose bumps to my skin.

The information about children at Bayview surprised me. I settled back against Bodey's side, staring off into the dusty trail behind us. Another vehicle followed, well back in the distance.

Who determined the worth of someone's soul? Who determined the value of a person? Freedom Pass had thrown or kept people based on their potential to serve the community. They'd controlled food and who went in and out. But Bayview had babies and a council to seek more people to share with. They wanted people, wanted to bring in as many as they could as long as they followed a moral and ethical code.

What made a group slip over the line? What made them choose to give up their souls for their lives or vice versa?

I glanced at Bodey. Just then the baby kicked and I allowed a sliver of hope to creep into my heart.

Maybe, just maybe, we could settle down and be together without someone chasing us, without fear that we wouldn't have a chance at warmth in the winter or food on our table. I didn't need stores or even TV. I swallowed. I could give up the toilets even, but I didn't want to lose my family or give up safety.

I could do anything, now that I knew how much I was worth.

My worth was incalculable.

Just like everyone else's.

EPILOGUE

Three years later

We'd found gloves in a small mercantile shop in Bayview. The owners sent out scavenging parties every week for more things to trade for. Our home was within Bayview boundaries but not so close we were inside town. I don't think we could handle that kind of community again.

The four bedroom rancher claimed its own space on the edge of the lake. Bodey and I lived with John and Dana, sharing the chore of gardening, cleaning, hunting, and living.

And raising Megan Jessica. She was a spitfire and didn't hold still long enough for just one or even two people to watch. We called her MJ for short. Usually she wasn't around for the second syllable of her name.

Almost three years old and her personality rivaled the most animated actresses I remembered seeing on television five or so years ago.

I sat back on my heels and watched as she blew dandelion fluff at Bodey, his answering grunt that she dare spread weeds around his corn patch enough to make her giggle and draw her grandparents' eyes.

A white flower on the creeping plants in the raised bed caught my eye. I whooped. "White flower! We're going to have a batch of strawberries, you guys!" The simple things were the big things now. I couldn't wait to see if we could find some sugar. Even honey from our bees would sweeten the berries like I remembered.

The front gate clattered shut. Bodey and John stood, hands rising to their side holsters. Whistling to us, Simon rounded the side of the house, hands in the air. He'd recovered nicely from his wounds, falling for the woman who'd nursed him back to health. They lived on the other side of town. He smiled. "Hey, how is my favorite family?"

"Uncle Simon." MJ squealed and ran into his arms.

Simon wasn't impervious to her charm and he threw her a few feet above him with a grin.

Holding her to his side, he turned and faced us, his eyes serious but with a happy undertone.

I stood and crossed the garden to stand beside Bodey. Whatever it was, we'd take it in stride. Together.

"We heard a message on the radio today." Simon's grin spread further into a full blown smile. "D.C. moved to Wichita, Kansas – well, what's left of it. From the conversation we had, it appears the Secretary of State is all that's left from the Oval Office. They are planning on rebuilding." He nodded at us as we exclaimed in disbelief. "I know. We're very excited. They want to call people to gather in areas of refuge until things get re-established – *tighter groups* is what they called it."

John, Dana, Bodey, and I glanced at each other and then at Simon, breaking into a round of laughter. A few seconds passed and our humor faded, dropping away to show our true emotions.

We'd learned enough about large groups to be wary. Even now, as much as we loved our home in Bayview, we regarded communities as dangerous and potential threats. Any place with too many members started to lower the value of the individual until only the group mattered.

"So I would like to offer you your choice of any of the empty homes closer to town, if not on a main street. You're a strong part of our community and we would love to have you in our midst on a more accessible basis." He patted MJ's back, watching us for our reaction.

Bodey reached for my hand, the warmth of his skin calming me. "If it's all the same to you guys, I'm good here. We've finally settled down. I don't need more of anything." He rubbed his fingers over my knuckles, the touch soft and simple, not sensual or even demanding, just a contact we both took for granted and loved all at the same time.

John nodded, pulling Dana in front of him and wrapping his arms around her. "We feel the same. We're here if you need us, but I think we have too much happiness in this place to share." He chuckled to lessen the sting, but his words rang true.

Simon inclined his head gently. "I thought as much, but I promised I'd offer and I wanted you to be one of the first to hear the news."

A collection of chairs by the deck drew us to sit down and talk.

I leaned over to Bodey, whispering as John and Simon laughed about a joke I'd heard at least ninety times since spring had arrived. "Do you really feel like you have enough? You don't want anything else?"

He slowly shook his head, placing a kiss on my lips and then touching his forehead to mine. "I'm perfectly happy. I don't need anything else."

I pursed my lips and drew my eyebrows together. "Well, what do I do with this baby, then? It's not like I can throw it back, you know?"

The group fell silent, and Bodey took a second as the news dawned on him. A smile split his lips, lighting his face. "A baby?" He breathed, his hands groping mine. "Another baby? Really?"

I nodded, tears gathering in my eyes. "I couldn't wait to tell everyone, but I wanted Simon here, too." I glanced at our visitor we thought of as an uncle. "It's about time. You haven't been here in a few weeks."

"I'm so glad I'm here now." He clapped his hands. "Well, this is just terrific. Along with celebrating a budding country, we get to celebrate the arrival of another soul."

A new soul whose worth had no measure.

Except potential.

I couldn't wait.

THE END

of *Worth of Souls*, read further for a letter from the author! Sign up for Bonnie's mailing list for first time access to short stories and novellas associated with the lives of people in the Worth of Souls series and for information about other upcoming releases.

Plus, enter contests and get excerpts, shorts, and so much more that is available **only** to her Survival Subscribers, please join Bonnie's survival mailing list so you'll be aware of her latest releases and get all kinds of fun survival tips! Come be a **SURVIVOR**!

For a list with covers and descriptions as well as links to all of Bonnie's other works please visit www.bonnierpaulson.net.

Bonnie R. Paulson is all about survival. Do you have what it takes to turn the page?

Find Bonnie at
Twitter: @bonnierpaulson
Facebook: http://facebook.com/bonpaulson
www.bonnierpaulson.net
bonnierpaulson@bonnierpaulson.net
You Tube

Visit me at
Www.BonnieRPaulson.net
Join my Survivor Newsletter
http://www.bonnierpaulson.net/#!subscribe-to-survival-in-bonnies-world/c21y3

Dear Survivor,

We made it. I can breathe easier.

This series has been the hardest for me to write from many different aspects. On one hand, the emotional draw was significant. I enjoyed the setting, the characters, the plot, everything was amazing – except when I lost a character. That was hard and I hated it.

Their reunion was my favorite thing to write in the entire series. I loved it so much. I hope you did, too.

The actual writing part of this series couldn't have been more trying. From moving twice in three months, to a broken finger, multiple sicknesses both myself and my family, opportunities to serve that, even though they cut severely into my writing time, I couldn't turn down.

There is a lot to be said about surviving alone versus surviving with friends. I've had a lot of help in that area and I'm grateful for the people I've met and known, both new and old family and friends.

As my reader, I hope you feel appreciated. I am grateful for you and for your time. Out of all the books out there, you picked my story to curl up with. I hope it has been an adventure and I hope you'll tell your friends about it.

If you have an extra moment, please stop by the site you purchased this story from and leave the book an honest review. Reviews are love to an author.

Thank you again so much. Please join my newsletter and I look forward to seeing you further. Hugs, my friend.

Stay Alive,
Bonnie R. Paulson